# The Truth Lies

## A Novel

Christopher Stoddard

Cuban Skies
5738 Masters
Orlando, Florida  32819
www.cubanskies.com

Cataloging-in-publication data is on file with the Library of Congress.

ISBN 0-9741452-0-3

Printed in the United States of America

First Edition

To my wife Sarah Jane,
and to the real Dan and Maria.

*Yo soy un hombre sincero*
*De donde crecen las palmas*
*Y antes de morirme quiero*
*Echar mis versos del alma*


*I am a sincere man*
*From where the palm trees grow*
*And before I die*
*I wish to share these verses*
*Which come from deep in my soul*


*Translated by Miguel and Nydia De La Hoz*
*Based on a poem by José Marti*

# ACKNOWLEDGEMENTS

Thanks to my wife and daughter and family and friends for their unwavering support and belief in me. Thanks to the real Dan and Maria for presenting the opportunity. Thanks to Maria Hinds for her advice early in the project. Thanks to Linda Baldwin for some great copy editing. Thanks to Bill Paskert and Ed Hooker for answering a couple technical questions. And thanks to Dan Duncan for a thorough read and, as always, many insightful comments.

Orlando, Florida
April 2003

# Chapter One

It was impossible to see through the darkness and rain. Gripping the handrail, Dan ventured below and stared intently at the screen of the global positioning system and the outline of the coast of Cuba a hundred yards from their boat.

"We're here," Dan shouted up to Alberto, who only nodded curtly in acknowledgement from the helm, trying to remain steady despite the violent rocking and pitching movements of the boat. Alberto reached into a compartment under the bench and took out what appeared to Dan to be oversize binoculars, but he soon recognized them as night vision goggles. Alberto put them on and peered toward the beach for several moments.

Reluctantly, he took them off. "I don't see them," he said. "It's 15 minutes past the rendezvous time." He handed the night vision goggles to Dan, who was about to put them away when Alberto suddenly shouted, "Over there!"

Dan saw only darkness as the rain pelted his face. After a moment, he could detect a small dim light flash three times, then two, then one. Alberto pointed his flashlight toward the

1

pinprick of light that emerged and returned the signal. He shouted to Dan, "Get the life vests!" as he gunned the engines and the boat surged toward the unseen shoreline.

The forward thrust nearly knocked Dan off his feet as he reached down to gather up the vests. Alberto cut the throttle, leaving the boat heaving wildly in the waves again. Dan could barely make out shapes wading into the surf toward the boat, as storm waves crested over them.

Dan heaved the rope ladder over the side into the face of a wave. He was already drenched, despite his foul-weather gear. The first person thrust into his arms was a child. A girl? Six or seven years old, fragile, skinny. He lifted her on board. Alberto strapped her into a life vest and pointed her below deck toward the stack of blankets waiting on a bench.

Two more children followed, then a teenage boy, and finally the parents. The doctor was the last one pulled on board, out of breath and gasping. Dan put a life vest on him and pulled in the ladder. Alberto gunned the engines and swung the boat around heading out to sea again. There was no time to lose.

One child was crying and the mother threw up, having swallowed too much salt water. Now that they were moving again things were better, but the rain was relentless and the waves continued to grow, cresting over the bow of the boat. The storm was getting worse. Dan didn't like the look of it, but he had put his trust in Alberto before.

Holding the handrail tightly, he watched as Alberto approached the waves at an angle instead of head on, riding the valleys between the crests. Alberto turned to Dan and pointed below. Dan knew what he meant. Steadying himself, he half-walked, half-crawled down the ladder to check the radar. To avoid detection, they turned it on for a few seconds at a time, and only when necessary.

Dan stared at the green screen for a moment, then switched it off. Not believing what he had just seen, he did it again. He held his breath as he watched the sweeping line complete a revolution and saw a blip near the center of the circle that indicated their boat's position. Turning the radar off, he shouted to Alberto, "There's another boat! It's almost on top of us!"

Alberto jerked his head around, quickly looking in all directions. Then he saw it, a dark shape speeding directly toward them some 50 yards away. No lights, like them. Not a good sign. Boats run without lights when they don't want to be seen. The captain either didn't know they were there, or didn't want them to know they had company. No one in his right mind would be out in this weather unless he was involved in some high-risk game.

Alberto let go of the wheel, bent down and opened a compartment. He took out a high-powered rifle and thrust

3

it into Dan's hands. They had discussed this scenario, but hoped it would never happen.

"Make damn sure you shoot them before they shoot us!" yelled Alberto.

Dan steadied the rifle as best he could in the pitching boat. He wiped the splattering rain from his eyes and looked through the night scope. The distance between the boats was quickly diminishing. It was hard to tell if the other boat was purposely aiming at them or not. It seemed like it, but there was no telling for sure in this sea.

"Dammit, amigo, they're going to run us down!" shouted Alberto as he turned the wheel and gunned the engines.

Dan steadied himself. He could feel the blood pounding at his temples as the boat pitched in the relentless waves. The scene felt suddenly surreal, as if he were removed from the situation.

Dan, an avowed pacifist, had never fired a weapon to harm anything. His sole experience with a gun was on a firing range where Alberto had showed him how to use the rifle he was now holding. He switched off the safety and slowly focused the sight at the oncoming boat.

"If you're on my boat in the open sea, you need to know how to use a rifle," Alberto had said. "It's one of life's realities."

The night vision scope on the rifle was good, as was the range of magnification. Alberto insisted on the best tools and equipment. If he couldn't buy quality, he would do without.

Seconds seemed like minutes as Dan peered down the scope. He wondered what he would do if he saw a rifle pointing back at him. Again, he tried to steady himself. His fingers were cold and cramped slightly as he zoomed in. He kept his trigger finger straight so as not to fire by mistake. He focused, but what he saw through the scope made no sense.

The person in the crosshairs was Maria. He recognized her instantly, even cloaked in a rain suit. There were several other people huddled in the cockpit of the boat with life vests on. What were the chances, he thought, of two boats making a run to Cuba on the same night, at the same time, to identical pickup points?

"They're not smugglers!" he yelled to Alberto as he lowered the rifle. "It's another boat of refugees! I know someone on the boat! It's Maria!"

"Damn luck!" yelled Alberto. He switched on the running lights and quickly turned his boat into an approaching wave, trying to run parallel to the approaching vessel. The wave ripped over the hull and smashed into Dan, knocking the rifle out of his hands. It skidded across the deck and off the benches, but did not discharge.

Dan tried to pull himself up, but his feet slipped. He fell and the back of his head bounced against the cockpit wall. Stunned, he shook his head and tried to focus.

That's when he saw it was too late to turn. The other boat was only yards away. Maria was holding onto the railing. She pushed one of the refugees down in the seconds before they collided.

The boats hit on an angle. The bow of Alberto's boat cut into the other vessel. Then a huge wave jerked them upward, suspending them above the other boat. Time and motion seemed suspended, as well—a split second dominated by nothing but the force of the wind, the waves, the driving rain.

In that instant, Dan wondered what the hell Maria was doing out here. She should be sitting at her desk back at the *Herald*. Seeing her on the other boat was so out of context, his brain couldn't process it. Another wave hit, again raising them over the other boat. Dan looked down, and saw Maria's face staring back at him, eyes wide, teeth clenched. Then he felt the boat plunge, felt the crash, and then… darkness.

He came to, sprawled on the deck and coughing up sea water. He could hear screams, but couldn't tell where they were coming from. Slowly, he dragged himself up and saw what was left of the other boat. The last wave had brought them down on top of it. He heard Maria shouting, "Dan! Dan!" She was beside their boat. He threw down the ladder, leaned over and pulled her from the water. He felt the lean, tense muscles in her arms as he hoisted her on board.

"They're out there! Help them!" she gasped, trying to regain her breath. He could see their shapes bobbing amidst the debris from the other boat. Dan stripped off his foul-weather gear and dove into the cold salt water. He grabbed the first person he found. He cradled the man's head as a lifeguard would, and slowly made his way back toward Alberto's boat. Maria was at the railing. She reached down to help pull the man on board. They kept going until Dan, exhausted, climbed back on the boat and collapsed in a heap beside Maria.

"How many?" he asked, breathing heavily. "How many did you have on board?"

"Six," she answered, "plus the captain."

"We're still missing a person," said Dan, looking at her tensely.

The storm kept pounding their boat, drenching them. The engine was dead, giving the waves even more power. The other boat had disappeared as if it had never been there. Dan and Maria peered desperately into the churning water, hoping to spot the missing person. They saw no one.

In the chaos, it took Dan several minutes to realize that Alberto was not at the helm. Dan struggled to his feet and spun around. No Alberto. Frantically, he flung open the cabin door and stumbled below only to find more refugees. No Alberto.

Dan climbed back up on deck. He yelled, "Alberto!" again and again as the waves rocked the boat. He moved from railing to railing, searching the blackness and shouting. Maria joined him, and together they scanned the surrounding waters.

Alberto was gone, vanished. When had it happened, screamed Dan to himself? When they crashed down onto the other boat? Probably—the force of that collision had knocked Dan out.

In a panic, Dan dove back into the water, despite Maria's protests. He swam through the flotsam and waves, spitting up seawater, looking for Alberto, looking for anyone. He swam around the boat until finally, almost too exhausted to pull himself back on board even with Maria's help, he lay gasping on the deck.

"We need to get the boat moving," Maria said tersely. "If it capsizes, we *all* die."

Dan nodded. Maria made her way to the helm and pulled herself up on the wheel. She tried the key. No response. She tried the running lights, but they didn't work either. The main battery is dead, she thought.

She went below and noticed at least a couple inches of seawater on the floor. Dan followed her, and together they assessed the grim situation. Dan opened a panel behind the ladder, struggled for a few seconds and managed to find the switch to the auxiliary power supply. The cabin lights came on, dimly, but they were on.

Dan climbed back up to the helm and tried the engine switch himself. It turned over, sputtered, then died. He tried again. Finally, it caught. He moved the throttle forward, and slowly the boat began to move. Only one of the engines was running and the boat was listing to the starboard side, but it was enough—hopefully enough to take them home.

He turned, and Maria was beside him. Their arms found each other. They kissed, then hugged fiercely, sharing tears and feeling raw emotions that neither of them fully understood.

# Chapter
# Two

Three days before Christmas, Miguel Montoro stood in line with his family at the airport in Havana and wondered if he was about to make the biggest mistake of his life.

His wife, Nydia, tried to dry her eyes with the handkerchief offered by Uncle Vicente, who had driven them in his ancient Chevrolet from Aunt Myriam's house on Calle San Julio. Although frail, the retired judge was dressed immaculately in his white suit and, as always, he stood erectly.

The children stayed close, avoiding the throngs of people in the airport lobby. Earlier that morning Nydia had instructed them to put on layers of clothing. In one pocket she slipped an old photograph, in another pocket she placed a rosary or some other small heirloom. It was all they had left. The boys, Miguelito and Alejandro, had grudgingly acquiesced to her wishes. Maria, however, had insisted on wearing only her one remaining dress for her journey to America.

Miguel looked at his young daughter in her white dress with her long dark hair neatly braided, and he wondered how it had come to this moment.

He paused, and in his mind's eye saw her riding a horse as if she had been born on one as she crested the hillside and made her way across the pastures to the town of Victoria de las Tunas. He realized it was a scene he might never see again.

The Montoro family was one of the oldest in the province. They had lived and worked in Las Tunas for generations, raising cattle and growing sugar cane. Although their plantation was of moderate size, it was well kept and its perimeters respected.

There were those in the village who thought Maria inherited her beauty from her mother, and there were others who would tell you she was the image of her grandmother as a young girl. Only the very oldest would tell you that her spirit and fierce determination reminded them of her great-grandmother.

Miguel was known in the province as an honest and fair man. He paid his workers every week and prayed with them on Sundays, along with his wife and children, in the church called "Verbo Incarnado" or "The Word Made Flesh." It was an old church with an even older legend.

It was said that a Spaniard named Alonso de Ojeda wrecked his ship off the coast of Cuba in 1519 and managed to escape with only his life and a statue of the Virgin Mary.

Happy to reach the shore alive, he made a vow that he would give the statue to the first village he came upon in honor of the Virgin Mary. His path carried him to an Indian village, Cueyba, where he sought out the local chief, gave him the statue and offered to help build a church in honor of Mary's divinity.

The school Maria attended stood next to that ancient church where the Montoro family worshiped and in the church was the statue of the Virgin Mary. Life in Victoria de las Tunas, formerly called Cueyba, was one rich in traditions handed down over centuries. It was in this peaceful and happy environment that Maria had grown up.

Miguel remembered the day in 1959 when it all changed, when Fidel Castro and the "Movimiento 26 de Julio" came to power. The corrupt Fulgenico Batista had fled the country on New Year's Eve, and Castro, when he arrived in Havana the next week, was cheered across the country as a hero. Even in Las Tunas, some had referred to him as *el Máximo Líder*, the Maximum Leader.

Many celebrated the long-awaited rebirth of democracy in a country that had seen more than its share of colonialism, corruption and terror. Father Mendez, the local priest, had high hopes for Castro and his army. He had seen the rosaries they wore over their olive-green uniforms when they paraded through the streets of Havana. Even those who may not have trusted or supported Castro shrugged their shoulders as if to say nothing could be worse than Batista; and now they were rid of him, so life could only become better.

That year did indeed bring many changes, but throughout its course, a painful truth became evident. As the months wore on, the new revolution wreaked havoc on every institution in the country. Governmental departments were chaotically reorganized, laws were changed or rewritten or ignored, and officials who raised objections were branded as traitors to the revolution and quickly arrested and imprisoned. As his Nydia put it, "It was as if God had looked down on us, but then walked away."

The promise of democracy and free elections was never fulfilled. Instead, revolutionary courts were established to prosecute hundreds of Batistianos, former supporters of Batista. Most were condemned to death and executed. Revenge became the first priority of the new regime.

Cheers were soon replaced by silence, but Castro did not initially move to outright censorship. It began more subtly, usually among friends and acquaintances. The new regime established its presence through "Revolutionary Councils" in each city and town across the country. Suddenly it was important how one was perceived in relationship to the revolution, and how dedicated one was to accepting the hardships and work necessary to achieve the goals of the party.

Miguel knew that if he were seen as less than enthusiastic about the current regime, he would soon be considered a person not to be associated with. If he were outright critical, the penalties could be much worse.

Despite official denials, there were persistent rumors that Castro was quickly moving away from democracy and toward communism. The editor of the local newspaper, José Chavez, had reported that Che Guevara himself authorized the seizure of all records from the headquarters of Cuba's anticommunist police force in Havana. Soon afterward, its Deputy Director was arrested and shot. José had also reported that several prominent communist movement leaders had quietly returned to Havana.

But then José disappeared, too, having fled Las Tunas and gone into hiding before being arrested. He had become a victim, like many other editors of newspapers, large and small, across Cuba. Publications printing remarks critical of the government, or any of its new policies, were branded as "counterrevolutionary." One by one, they were destroyed through various techniques. There were staged union demonstrations and sometimes violent mobs orchestrated by the Castro regime. Eventually there was an eerie uniformity to everything one heard or read in the newspapers, on radio, or television. The message was that the revolution was great and that one must be obedient and serve the great cause.

After the media was silenced, the churches and schools were next on the agenda of Castro's increasingly repressive regime, and his reach extended even to Las Tunas. When Maria rode her horse into town on a morning in early 1959, Father Mendez was not there to greet her as he always did and help her off the horse with his usual greeting, "And how are you this morning, my little Maria? Are you prepared to learn today?"

Other young students had also gathered outside the school next to the ancient church, but the doors were closed and several soldiers stood outside with guns.

On a regular morning, they would listen to Father Mendez read a history book aloud followed by religious instruction. The older children would then study math problems, while the youngest, like Maria, would draw pictures and learn alphabet letters.

The lesson plan that day would be far different. One of the army soldiers opened the doors and instructed the children to enter the building in single file. Father Mendez addressed them in the gymnasium with four soldiers standing by his side. His face was taut and haggard.

"My children," he said, "I must introduce you to your new teachers, as I will no longer be able to instruct you because of other duties I have been asked to perform to support the cause of the revolution. From now on you will be instructed by Señora Manuel."

A stern-faced young woman in a khaki uniform stepped forward and nodded curtly at the assembled students. She began by telling them about their great responsibilities to the cause of the revolution and how it was necessary that they pledge their allegiance and loyalty to it.

"There will no longer be any need for religious instruction," she continued. "You will be far too busy putting your full-time efforts into your studies. You will be asked to do much more than has been asked of you in the past. The cause demands it and our Maximum Leader asks you to meet the challenge. While you may think you are but children, in reality you are the next generation of the revolution, and you must be ready to take on that great responsibility."

The older students were asked to give written answers to questions about their friends and families. Señora Manuel wanted to know curious kinds of information, like what kind of car their parents drove; did they have a television or radio in their home; and what sort of books and newspapers their parents read.

Later, there would be other questions about their parents and relatives, and anything they might have heard them say about the government, or about their beliefs, or their commitment to the revolution. Rewards were promised in the form of gold stars to be stitched on one's shirt or blouse for those students who volunteered to become proud *Pioneros*, or young pioneers. Señora Manuel reminded them, "It is for all our benefit so that we can be better instructed and therefore better citizens."

Father Mendez put up with these intrusions for as long as he could before breaking his silence. Two Sundays later he read aloud a letter from the Monsignor in Havana to a church that was less than half full. In a strong voice, Father Mendez read the Monsignor's protests about the aggression to which the church was being subjected. He described schools being taken over or closed, and priests and nuns being forced to leave Cuba, or sometimes arrested and imprisoned. He spoke of university professors being forced to resign and student governments being banned and their leaders jailed.

Father Mendez finished the letter and looked out at the faces of his diminished parish and made his own plea. "What is happening here and across our country is wrong," he said. "We must speak out. To remain in silence is a lie. To repeat the lies that are forced upon us is an even greater sin. Please join me in prayer," and he recited the Our Father. The Montoro family, sitting in the second pew from the front on the left side of the church, recited the prayer with him.

Within two days, Father Mendez was detained by the police and quickly disappeared from public view. Later, it would be announced that he had been officially charged with "counterrevolutionary activities" and, presumably, taken to prison. Miguel, with several other influential citizens, had strongly protested the arrest, but their efforts had no results other than the fact that their names were duly entered on a list kept by the local Committee for the Defense of the Revolution.

Soon after the "detainment," Maria had asked her father the obvious question, "What happened to Father Mendez? Why did the soldiers take him away?"

Miguel had paused before replying, then lifted young Maria into his arms and sat down with her on his lap. Gently stroking her hair, he told her that Father Mendez was a man of God who spoke the truth, and that it was very unjust that he had been arrested. He told Maria that he and others had tried to help, but could not, and that now they could only pray for his safety. Maria, though disappointed, accepted his answer as the way it would have to be.

He still recalled bitterly when, a few months later, the revolutionary army captain had showed up at their doorstep demanding that he appear before the provincial headquarters of the Agrarian Reform Institute the next week. Castro had formed the organization in May of that year, and gave it broad, sweeping powers to seize land and property with the stated purpose of redistributing it to newly formed "co-operatives."

"The cruel joke," Miguel had pointed out to Nydia, "is that workers still don't own the land; the co-operatives do. They pay less than I did and offer nothing but empty promises of future wealth. Castro's truths are nothing but lies!"

Miguel's appearance before the tribunal was perfunctory. He sat alone across a table from five uniformed "officers" who informed him that an inventory would be made of his property and the land redistributed to his workers based on a "master plan."

Miguel had considered arguing, but realized his words would have no sway given the preposterous disposition of the tribunal.   Controlling his emotions, he returned to the plantation that had been in their family for so many years, and told his wife and his children the news.

Initially, only a portion of the Montoro family's machinery, livestock, and property was seized, but it was a sure sign of what was to come.  There were other indications, too.  In July Castro forced Cuban President Urrutia out of office and appointed a Marxist lawyer, Osvoldo Dorticó to the position. In November one of the last remaining liberals in the government, Filip Pazos, was replaced by Che Guevara as president of the National Bank.

By early 1960, Castro's path toward communism had become clear to all.  With much pomp and circumstance, he greeted Soviet Deputy Premier Anastas Mykoyan on his first official visit to Cuba.   Mykoyan committed the USSR to purchase five million tons of sugar from Cuba with generous credit allowances.  It was the beginning of a long and costly financial arrangement with Cuba.

There remained a few pockets of resistance in the Cuban populace, mostly among Catholic activists and within the university communities, but Castro had consolidated his hold on the centers of power within the country.

Faced with this turn of events, people began to leave Cuba.

It started with the educated professionals, and then the entrepreneurs. Lines began forming at the U.S. Consulate in Havana. In the course of 1960 alone, some 60,000 fled to the United States, despite efforts by Castro to block them by canceling all exit visas and through outright intimidation. Families were separated. Desperate parents, fearing for the safety of their children, tried to find ways to get them out of Cuba. People started taking risks, and Miguel took note.

Across Cuba, land and property were being confiscated on a wholesale basis. It began with seizures of property and businesses belonging to Batistianos, former supporters of Batista, and spread to the media and private schools; by July of 1960, it included all British and U.S.-owned refineries. In a single 24-hour period in October, the Cuban government expropriated all U.S.-owned property and businesses totaling billions of dollars in investments and profits and jobs.

In Las Tunas, that October brought the final seizure of the plantation that the Montoro family had built and owned. They were relegated to only a portion of their former home. They lost the rest of their land, machinery, livestock, as well as many personal possessions. The land was "redistributed" through the co-operative to the former employees.

It had been only through his workers' quiet allegiance and generosity that Miguel Montoro was able to feed and clothe his family during that sad period. Taking turns, the workers secretly paid tribute to their former employer. A sack of vegetables would be left on the doorstep. An occasional ham would appear. These acts of kindness would usually take place in the late evenings, when the watchful eyes of the local Committee for the Defense of the Revolution were less likely to observe.

With the state controlling the newspapers, radio and television stations, only news authorized and approved by the Castro regime was allowed to be broadcast or published. The government had come to effectively control almost every aspect of the citizens' lives, from determining what one heard to what one was allowed to eat to where one lived. The government decided where one would work, how much one would be paid, and how one should spend that paltry amount of money.

Finally, the government attempted to control ideas, for as Miguel knew, they were the most dangerous threat to any totalitarian state. The party determined which ideas were noble and patriotic, and which were evil and should be condemned. This censorship extended beyond books and magazines and periodicals. Simple spoken words could now make one a suspect. A conversation might be overheard and reported. Blind allegiance was encouraged and rewarded; dissension was punished harshly.

Miguel Montoro, who had hoped for the best, now braced himself for the worst. He knew that his family's days in Cuba were numbered. As impossible as it seemed for them to leave

Las Tunas and all that they had worked over generations to achieve, it was evident that even the little left to them after the revolution would also be taken away eventually.

They now lived in only three rooms of what used to be their plantation home. "The house is far too large for one family," the Committee for the Defense of the Revolution representative had said. "Three families can easily live under this roof." In the small space they were now occupying, the Montoro family began the process of saying good-bye to the world they had known. They sorted through what material possessions were still left, discarding most. Only the most precious family photos and keepsakes remained, those things they held closest to their hearts.

With the money they had left, Miguel planned to arrange exit visas for them. He knew it would take time and that it would not be cheap. What little extra cash might be left over, if any, he would smuggle out to friends or family in America or Mexico.

Miguel now remembered walking outside and standing alone on the porch of his former home one night after the rest of the family had gone wearily to sleep. He recalled gazing at the nighttime sky while he tried to chart a new course for himself and for his family.

Uncle Vicente leaned over and kissed each of the children and hugged Nydia before saying good-bye to Miguel.

"I do not think we will meet again," he said shaking his hand.

"Do not say such a thing, Uncle Vicente. Of course we will," replied Miguel. But he could see in the old man's eyes that this good-bye was somehow final. Vicente nodded and released Miguel's hand, then slowly made his way across the crowded airport lobby.

Ahead of them was the glass-enclosed area called "the fishbowl" that housed the customs and passport control stations. It was the final checkpoint through which all departing passengers had to pass.

"We must be careful not to be separated," Miguel said as he looked nervously about the terminal. There were many guards, most of them armed, stationed throughout the building. The long lines were confusing, with everyone shuffling for position, but seemingly never moving ahead. When they did move, there were abrupt halts for 20 or 30 minutes at a time. More unnerving was the fact that every now and again, guards would approach passengers, sometimes questioning them; other times pulling them out of line and taking them away for no apparent reason.

Miguel looked up and suddenly noticed a guard standing in front of him.

"I said women only in this line," the guard repeated. "The men go over there."

"But we are a family." said Miguel. "We are together."

The guard merely shrugged and pointed to a line consisting of only males on the other side of the room. Reluctantly, Miguel dug into his coat pocket and extracted the precious exit visas, carefully handing two of them to Nydia.

Nydia's breath quickened as she took the visas from Miguel and put them deep in her pocket. She could feel the few dollar bills she had sewn into the lining of her jacket with the hope that they would not be detected.

Maria sensed her mother's tension as Nydia's grip tightened on her small hand. The last days had been a blurred adventure to Maria. They had left Las Tunas early in the morning two days before with little packing required, for they had already given away or sold most of their jewelry and personal effects long before the immigration interview.

The "interview" had taken the better part of half a day and was really more of an interrogation. The officer had many questions. He wanted to know exactly who the child's parents talked to in Las Tunas and what they talked about. Maria thought it odd that he knew exactly what days and times her mother went to church.

Finally, the telegram confirming that their papers had been approved arrived. Once the departure date and flight had been set, they said good bye to a few trusted friends. For the most part, their departure would go unannounced. The fewer that knew the better. Like so many others before, they would quietly take their leave and disappear.

Of the two trains that ran to Havana each day from Las Tunas, they took the morning departure. The ten-hour trip would bring them to Havana in the evening.

The morning they left Las Tunas, Maria awoke early having heard the front door open and close. She dressed quickly and in the pre-dawn darkness she followed her father as he took a solitary walk across the land that his family had farmed for so many generations. He stopped midway in a field between two long rows of cane, bent down, and picked up a handful of dirt. He rubbed it in his hand, the fertile soil that had been so good to him and to his family. Then he brushed his hands on his pants and took a long look around one last time. When he turned, he was surprised to find Maria standing behind him.

"What are you doing, Papi?" she asked.

"I'm just saying good-bye," he said.

After departing Las Tunas, the train traveled through the province of Camagüey, Cuba's largest and most sparsely populated. From there it took them through Sancti Spíritus and Santa Clara. In the late afternoon it pulled into Matanzas, about 65 miles east of Havana, where it stopped for 15 minutes. Maria and her family got out and stretched, as did the rest of the passengers, weary and stiff from a day of traveling.

"What will happen when we reach Havana, Papi?" asked Maria.

"Don't worry," he answered, "we will stay with your great aunt." Though he tried not to show it, Maria could see her father was both distracted and worried.

It was dusk when they arrived in Havana. From the train station, they took a city bus across town to Miguel's aunt's home. Traffic was congested on the old and crowded streets. Horns honked, brakes screeched. Near the center of the city, the bus had just rounded a corner when there was a loud crash. The car ahead of them had attempted to proceed through the intersection, only to hit an army jeep that had run the red light. The two soldiers in the jeep immediately jumped out and began shouting at the man in the car.

Maria, sitting in a window seat of the bus, leaned out and could see the jeep was only one in a caravan that included four jeeps and an aging but highly polished Mercedes limousine. Other soldiers had now clustered around the car and the first jeep that had caused the collision. There was much shouting and waving of hands.

Suddenly, the back door of the limousine flew open, and Maria's eyes grew wide. *El Comandante* himself stepped out onto the cobblestone pavement. He wore his usual green khaki's, but no hat. A revolver was strapped to his shiny black belt. He was taller than Maria had imagined from his pictures in the newspapers.

Castro fiercely gestured at the civilian vehicle and uttered a terse two-word command to the nearest soldier, "Remove it!"

Two more military vehicles had now screeched to a halt, and the intersection was suddenly crowded with Castro's elite guard. The civilian driver was summarily hauled out of his car to the side of the street and beaten by two of the soldiers before being thrown into the back of their jeep. No less than a dozen soldiers then converged on the car. Heaving and pushing, they separated the vehicles. Then they lifted the civilian's car and rolled it onto its side, opening a path for the motorcade.

Castro climbed back in the limousine and slammed the door. The motorcade sped off as Maria continued to stare from the window before the bus, too, proceeded on its path.

They got off the city bus at the corner of Calle San Julio and walked the short distance to Aunt Myriam's home. A stately old white house with a tile roof, it had originally belonged to her sister, Miguel's grandmother.

When they arrived at the door, Miguel paused. He had not talked to his aunt, a pharmacist, in some months. She had chosen to be an active member of the Communist party. It was difficult for him to call and seek her aid, but she had graciously accepted their request to spend their last couple nights in Cuba under her roof. He knocked once and his Aunt Myriam, a tall thin woman, opened the door and beckoned them inside.

She hugged each of them in turn until she came to Miguel. She took his hands and looked at him closely before saying, "Are you sure this is what you want to do, Miguel? You know that by leaving, you will perhaps never be able to return." He nodded and she hugged him closely. "Okay then," she said, "let me fix you something to eat."

Miguel knew he was putting Myriam in a precarious situation. While they still cared deeply about each other, politics had divided the family, as happened to many families in Cuba. To have a relative leave Cuba was considered a disgrace to a party member and the less said about it, the better. Miguel knew their pending departure had deeply hurt her pride, but he was grateful she respected his decision to leave Cuba.

"Thank you again for this kindness you do for me and my family," he said, but she would hear none of it.

"We are all part of the same family, and families are important, even in the revolution," she added resolutely.

None of them slept well that night. Nydia and Miguel shared a single bed while Maria and her brothers lay on top of their sweaters on the floor of the bedroom. With their departure only a day away, the reality that they were leaving and most likely would never return, sank in. Nydia was so distraught and emotionally fatigued that when sleep finally did come, she stayed in bed much of the next day. A concerned Aunt Myriam gave her a vitamin B shot in an effort to rejuvenate her.

Late in the afternoon of their last day, Miguel took Maria and her brothers for a long walk through the streets of old Havana. Along the way, he pointed out the landmarks and tried to make a series of mental pictures that he could save and always remember. They walked the length of the tree-shaded promenade Paseo del Prado that started at Parque Central and stretched down to the Malecón sea wall. Her father bought them each a drink from one of the umbrella-covered concession stands and they stood at the sea wall and watched the breakwaters for a time as people on bicycles crisscrossed the plaza. The late afternoon sun caused the ornate facades and arches of the buildings behind them to take on tones of amber and gold.

Now Maria and her mother entered the glass-enclosed area, the "fish bowl." Miguel could see them from where he stood farther back in the other line with the boys. He silently prayed that they would all make it through this ordeal without being pulled out of the queue. He had no idea what happened to those who were approached by the guards, but he feared the worst. They were quickly ushered into various side rooms, and none that he saw taken away had reappeared.

Finally, he and the boys also entered the "fish bowl." There was no turning back now, as there were guards with guns both ahead of them and behind them. He held the exit visas tightly in his hands.

Maria and Nydia approached the inspection station, partially hidden by other people in the crowded line. Somebody bumped Miguel and he turned, then looked back, but Maria and Nydia were gone from his sight. He could only hope they had passed through the station with no incident.

As Miguel neared the inspection station, two guards appeared and demanded to see the papers of the man in front of him. They briefly glanced at the documents before pulling him out of the line and ushering him into a side door that they closed behind them.

Miguel was sweating as he handed the exit papers to the guard at the inspection station. Miguelito and Alejandro kept their eyes lowered and stood silently as the guard inspected the visas.

"How much money are you taking with you?" asked the guard addressing Miguel, who silently dug into his pocket and revealed a hundred pesos.

"These papers are not correctly stamped," said the guard. "You must pay a fee."

He took the hundred pesos from Miguel's hand, then stamped the visas and motioned them through the turnstile. Ahead of them was a long table with three more guards standing idly behind it. Miguel and his sons were asked to remove their sweaters and they were patted down and had their pockets searched.

They were allowed to keep the two framed photographs the guards found in the boys' pockets, but Nydia's mother's rosary was confiscated when they discovered it in Miguelito's pants pocket. Finally, though, they were allowed through the door exiting the glass room. Miguel felt dizzy and he put his hands on the boys' shoulders to steady himself as they entered the departure terminal.

He looked for Nydia and Maria among the crowds, then finally saw them. Maria ran to him in her white dress with Nydia behind her. He hugged them both as they made their way to the gate.

The plane, an aging DC-6, was parked on the tarmac. They had to climb a set of rusting stairs that had been rolled into place before the open cabin door.

Just before they entered the plane, Maria noticed Uncle Vicente standing alone on the balcony of the terminal. He slowly waved a white handkerchief, his thin frame silhouetted against the blue morning skies. She returned his wave.

The cabin was crowded and they could not all sit together. The two turboprops sputtered to life loudly and the plane taxied to the end of the runway. It made a sharp U-turn and then, at full throttle, lumbered back down the runway. Miguel would later remember the moment when the wheels lifted off the ground and they were no longer on Cuban soil more than he would recall the pilot's announcement when they left Cuban airspace and everyone clapped.

For a long time after they were airborne Miguel sat in silence holding his wife's hand.

"We must think of all that we have before us," he finally said. "We must think of the family and friends who have already made this journey and will be waiting for us when we arrive."

Leaning back in his seat and closing his eyes, Miguel felt a great loss mixed with the anticipation of the new life before them. There was no turning back. The life they had led was over. It felt like death and rebirth to him. The lives that their families had built over generations in Cuba were finished and buried. This was their new course, their new life. They would arrive in Miami, in America, to begin again.

# Chapter Three

Nydia stared out the window of the DC-6 as the aging plane flew over Havana's harbor. As she looked down at *La Cabaña*, the ancient Spanish fortress Castro used as a prison, the image of Fernando García floated up to her. She thought of him as she watched the coast of Cuba, the country of her birth, grow smaller and smaller.

Even after all the dramatic changes in their lives thrust upon them and their country by Castro's regime, Nydia and Miguel held on to the slim hope of remaining in Cuba. After all, there were still those who believed that Castro's regime would not last. Even those who had fled Cuba anticipated soon returning, their stay in Miami or Mexico being just a temporary residence.

Among those who chose to stay in Cuba, however, there were some who quietly talked of a new regime, of an end to Castro's tyranny, and the advent of a true democracy. One such person was Fernando García, an old business acquaintance of Miguel's.

Miguel traveled one day to Santiago de Cuba on the southeast coast at the foothills of the Sierra Maestra Mountains to speak with Fernando. His friend's house was outside the city on a hillside. A well-educated man, Fernando's interests included property, business and politics. Although in his 60s, he was still fit and healthy. Fernando personally met Miguel at the door of his hacienda and ushered him to the glass-enclosed sunroom. There were no servants to be seen. He was alone and the house seemed empty.

"I know things have not been well for you, or for many of us, my old friend," Fernando said. "Sit, please sit. I'll get us something to drink and we can talk. The servants are all gone I'm afraid, as well as many friends."

He left the room but soon returned carrying a carved wooden platter with a pitcher of *Mojito* and two glasses on it. The two old friends sat and talked through the afternoon. Miguel told him of the loss of his land and plantation, the arrest and disappearance of Father Mendez, the takeover of the school, and his ultimate decision that he and his family would leave Cuba after he could arrange for exit visas.

Fernando listened attentively but said nothing. Finally, he leaned forward when Miguel had finished and said, "I know you have come to me for advice as to how best to leave the country, and I do know of ways that can be done, but I beg of you not to do so, my friend. There is much afoot at this time." Fernando spoke slowly in a low voice telling Miguel of plans that were underway. He told him of the counterrevolutionary forces that had already been formed. He told him how the United States had agreed to train and prepare the troops for the overthrow of Castro, now that the former cordial relationship between Cuba and the United States had been completely severed.

Rumors of such activities were not uncommon at that time, but Fernando knew details to which only someone in an inner circle of dissidents would have access. He described the development of a strong guerrilla army consisting of exiled patriots who were training, even as they spoke, at a secret location on the West Coast of Guatamala, near Retalhueleu. He spoke of the support the United States had supplied, including the ships that would sail from Puerto Cabezas in Nicaragua, loaded with troops, equipment and munitions.

The force would land at various points around the island under the protection of U.S. B-26 bombers. Multiple Cuban airfields would be attacked simultaneously and Castro's air force would be crippled. "The planes will be disguised," said Fernando, "to appear as if they were from Castro's own fleet flown by defecting pilots. America has committed to help us, but its leaders cannot show their hand.

"With their help, we will overthrow this devil Fidel Castro, and take back our country. We will no longer have to pretend that his lies are truths," said Fernando. "My own son plays no small part in this mission," he finally offered proudly. "He will fight bravely beside many other young patriots. I only wish I were young enough to fight with them."

He refilled their glasses and said, "I ask you to hold on as long as you can, Miguel. This is our home and, to leave it, we admit defeat. We need people like you, leaders in the community and true patriots. America has guaranteed our victory. With their planes, the skies will be ours. And if we own the skies, we will win the war." Fernando smiled then, his cheekbones rising and accentuating the deep wrinkles in his face. His eyes gleamed like a zealot's.

Reluctantly, Miguel agreed to stay in Cuba. He returned to Las Tunas, to the plantation that was no longer his and the home that his grandfather had built in which three families now lived.

Since the plantation had been seized, Miguel had been relegated to the role of a common laborer. He spent his days working alongside his former employees on the plantation. He did not complain. The Committee however, as a final cruel gesture, decreed that Miguel should be paid less than any of the other workers, who already barely existed on the paltry sums they received for their labors. Miguel's wages could no longer feed a single person, much less a family, and they would have starved were it not for the late-night supplements left on their doorstep.

Miguel was about to retire on a late evening in early spring of 1961 when he thought he heard someone on the porch. It was less than a knock, really more of a quiet tap. He suspected it might be one of the workers leaving a food package. Upon opening the door, he was surprised to find Fernando García standing in the shadows.

"May I come in, my old friend?" asked Fernando.

Miguel quickly beckoned him inside, then cautiously glanced up and down the deserted street before closing the door.

"I was not seen or followed," said Fernando. "Do not worry."

They sat in the kitchen as there was nowhere else to sit. Nydia greeted Fernando warmly. If she was surprised by the visit, she did not show it, and immediately went about preparing coffee. Young Maria came in from the bedroom where she had been asleep. Stifling a yawn, she walked up to Fernando and gave him a hug before settling in her father's lap. Maria's two older brothers, Miguelito and Alejandro, heard the conversation and also came into the room, standing behind their father as he sat at the table.

They made small talk for a good while before Fernando paused, glanced cautiously around the room, and then at Miguel.

"There are no secrets within this family," Miguel assured him. "We understand the importance of what you are about to tell us, and will tell no one." They all nodded solemnly.

"I am meeting with resistance groups in the province," said Fernando. "The time is now close at hand. As our army lands and moves toward Havana, we will not only need the support of the local citizens, but also new soldiers, as many will surely die in this cause. I am an old man and cannot fight, but I can help pave the way for our army."

As Miguel nodded at his old friend sitting in the chair across from him, he noticed for the first time that the stress of the past weeks had taken its toll on him. Fernando had always looked younger than his years, but now he looked his age, perhaps older. He had acquired the habit of absently squeezing his hands together now and again while talking, moving his bony fingers back and forth. But his eyes were clear and fierce and his voice was strong and steady, as always.

Although Fernando remained optimistic about the operation, there were problems. With a new American President now in office, plans had been changed, and then changed again. Instead of a guerilla war that would be fought on multiple fronts, a single large-scale invasion was now planned. Instead of multiple sites, there was now only one landing point, and that location had just been changed, too.

"Our forces were to land at Trinidad-Casilda," he

continued, "a site my son José helped choose." He sighed. "Just today I learned it has been changed by the new American President to *Bahia de Cochinos*, the Bay of Pigs, near Girón.

"To be honest, I don't think much of the new location," said Fernando bluntly. "There are no mountains to retreat to, there is treacherous coral off the coastline, and only a miserable swamp nearby for landing." He sighed and took a sip of coffee.

"But make no mistake about it," he said finally, "our sons will succeed. Three days before the landing, air attacks will cripple Castro's air force on the ground. The CIA has already arranged for the aircraft and our pilots have been well trained."

"And after the landing, what then?" asked Miguel.

"Once the beachhead is established, our troops will march toward Havana. Our patriots will gain popular support as they march across the country. The people will rally them on. And any counteroffensive that Castro may contemplate will be crushed. He will face mass uprisings and desertions from his army and we will welcome any who come. There will be no retribution. At the end of the day, we will have Cuba back, my friend."

Fernando thumped his index finger on the table to

emphasize his strong belief that victory would be theirs. Maria and her brothers watched and listened, transfixed.

Finally, Miguel asked, "How can I help, Fernando? How can I help you in this effort?"

"Quietly talk to your men," said Fernando. "Tell them not to give up hope. Tell them a great army of patriots will soon arrive. Ask those among them who are able to consider joining its ranks."

"I will fight with them, Papi!" shouted Maria's oldest brother Miguelito. "Me, too!" joined in Alejandro, the middle child. Their mother quickly shushed them.

Fernando smiled briefly and said, "I am sorry, but you boys are far too young, although I commend your exuberance and bravery."

"I will gladly talk to the men," said Miguel finally, "but you must realize that I am only another worker these days. I am no longer anyone's boss. I no longer give orders."

"Nonsense," interjected Nydia, wiping her hands on her apron. "Those men cannot have greater respect for you. Any one of them would gladly die for you as quickly as he would his own brother. They will listen to you, Miguel. They always have. They always will."

Miguel nodded. He would talk to the workers. Fernando leaned forward and said, "Good. Then let me tell you when these great events are to take place..."

Some 400 miles away in the Presidential Palace in Havana, a solitary figure stood on the balcony overlooking the darkened plaza. Dressed in fatigues, only his outline could be seen against the lamplight of the room behind him. He stood with his arms crossed, facing the plaza. His cigar glowed in the shadows. Even in the darkness, the Maximum Leader could be mistaken for no one else.

Fidel Castro did not know all the details Fernando had shared with Miguel and his family, but he knew enough. There had been leaks in the press and his operatives had successfully infiltrated some of the ranks of these so-called "patriots," who he preferred to refer to as worms, or *gusanos*. While he did not know exactly when or where the attack would be staged, he did know of the plans to disable his air force. Made up largely of aircraft left behind by the Batista regime, but increasingly bolstered by Soviet weaponry consisting of heavy tanks, rocket launchers, and, importantly, antiaircraft guns, the air force was Castro's personal pride and the heart of his military forces.

Armed with knowledge of the plot, he had dispersed or hidden most of his prized aircraft and purposely left only obsolete or unusable planes visible on the airfields. These, he hoped, would act as decoys to draw the attention of the bombers. And then he would strike back.

Yes, he would be waiting for this army of exiles, these *gusanos* who bowed before a new American President too fearful to face Castro man-to-man, frightened that the world would see his true imperialistic intentions. A lesson needed to be taught here, and Castro, the Maximum Leader, would now become the Maximum Teacher in order to ensure the lesson was properly administered.

On April 14, 1961, as luck would have it, the same date the doomed ocean liner called the *Titanic* sank some four-and-a-half decades earlier, six ships left the Nicaraguan port city of Puerto Cabezas under cover of darkness. Bound for Cuba, they were laden with soldiers, guns, gasoline, and the equipment of war.

A young captain named José García stood at a railing as the convoy put out to sea carrying the expeditionary force that would become known as Brigade 2506. The thought of returning to his homeland as part of a liberating army lifted his heart. He knew how proud his father Fernando would be and he resolved to honor that which his father stood for and had worked to accomplish for so many years—a free and open Cuba. He knew their task would not be easy, but he was prepared to die in trying to accomplish it.

José had not been told, nor had any of the exile forces on board, that the task would be far more difficult due to the last-minute decision to change the landing location to the Bay of Pigs. The fact that they would have to attempt a landing at night made an already dangerous operation outright perilous.

He looked at the other young faces around him on the deck and found them determined, but not frightened. He knew the weight of the future of his nation was squarely on their shoulders, and they would carry it. They would succeed. They would bring freedom home.

As Fernando had predicted, at dawn on Saturday, April 15th, the air attack began when six ancient, slow-moving B-26 planes, disguised to look like they were being flown by defecting Cuban air force pilots, took off from Nicaragua.

It was not, however, the attack that had been anticipated. The battle plan had been changed again by the White House in a last minute revision, and only half the planes initially designated were actually sent.

President Kennedy had just proclaimed again publicly that there was no planned U.S. intervention in Cuba, and he was worried. To send in too many planes, he feared, might reveal the secret involvement of the United States and potentially damage its relations in Latin America and the world, through the United Nations. Perhaps it would be wiser, he thought, just to send in a few planes at first to make it look more like a small but growing uprising within the ranks of Castro's own air force. It proved to be a fatal mistake.

The lumbering planes, too few in number, and too slow in speed, managed to bomb only a handful of the airfields, and left Castro's main air force well intact.

Meanwhile, the efforts of the White House to keep the whole operation secret began to unravel. The rest of that April day would not go well for the Kennedys. As part of the complicated plan hatched by the CIA, two additional bombers had been assigned to fly from Nicaragua directly to the U.S. mainland and land in Miami and Key West, where the "defecting" pilots would claim they had come from Cuba and ask for asylum. The notion was that this would bolster the cover story that the invasion came from within the ranks of Castro's own forces.

The press, however, quickly picked apart the story. There were inconsistencies in the fabricated tale and the authenticity of the planes was challenged. A reporter noted the obvious difference that the noses of the disguised planes were solid, whereas actual Cuban air force bombers had clear plexiglass noses. Another wondered why the guns on the two planes were still covered, despite the pilots' claims they were attacked and had engaged in a furious gun battle in the course of their defection. The phones at the White House began ringing.

Although he had not yet heard of the initial air attacks, Castro was busy with his own preparations. He launched the most massive roundup of suspected individuals in the history of Cuba. Some 500,000 people were detained in towns and cities across the country, almost all of whom had committed no crime, nor played any part in the insurrection. Later, he would brag that he had learned from Batista's mistakes. Never take an enemy for granted and always suspect your own citizens. The local neighborhood committees had turned in their lists of suspects, and the internal security police worked overtime to hastily round up so many people. The "suspects" were summarily herded into makeshift concentration camps anywhere that they could be secured. They found themselves held captive in stadiums, theaters, and schools.

On that morning an armed soldier pounded on Miguel Montoro's door with the butt of his rifle. A flatbed truck with a haphazard screen of chicken wire stretched over the bed idled on the street with two more armed guards standing by it.

"Miguel Montoro, you are hereby detained by the state on the executive order of Fidel Castro, and will stay under detention until such time as you are exonerated. Get on the truck," barked the guard.

"What is this about?" protested Miguel, but the guard would hear none of it. He clenched Miguel's shirt and threw him to the ground in front of the house. Maria appeared in the doorway, and rushed to her father as he lay on the ground screaming "Papi, Papi!"

The two other guards dragged Miguel to the truck where they casually tossed him onto the flatbed and closed the wire door. A good portion of the other prominent citizens of Las Tunas had also been "detained" that morning, including all of those who, with Miguel, had protested the arrest of Father Mendez. He sat up to find himself surrounded by the familiar, but bruised and scratched, faces of old friends and acquaintances.

Nydia remembered how she ran up to the truck and stood by Maria. She reached out with one hand to the wire cage, looked into Miguel's eyes, and tried to smile. She willed herself to be calm despite the terror in her heart. She knew she had to be brave at this moment for him and for the children.

The truck pulled away, spewing diesel exhaust and raising dust. Maria broke away from her mother and chased it down the road until, out of breath, her mother finally caught her. Maria's brothers also rushed out into the road. They shouted at the truck as it drove away and damned Castro and his regime of lies. They cursed the guards who took away their father and searched for rocks, anything they could throw at the receding truck, which was already too far down the road to hit.

And then the truck was gone and it was oddly quiet, except

for Maria crying in her mother's arms in the middle of the road. Her older brothers stood on either side of them as if to protect them from the next truck, the next attack, or perhaps the next car that came upon them. But none came. They were alone and there was only silence, except for the ringing in their ears that only a raging heart can explain.

Sometime in the early hours of Sunday, April 16, six ships approached the Cuban mainland. U.S. Navy frogmen had already set up landing lights on the shore of the Bay of Pigs before departing to avoid detection. The liberating army consisted of 1,500 men divided into six battalions, half of which came ashore at Playa Girón and Playa Larga. The problems began almost immediately.

José García led his men onto a landing boat. In the darkness and confusion, it was quickly filled to capacity. As it motored toward the beach, he could hear guns firing and see flashes from the shore. Suddenly there was a loud scraping sound and the boat rocked on a steep angle.

The U-2 spy photos taken earlier of the bay had shown large dark patches that the U.S. advisors had interpreted and dismissed as masses of seaweed. They were, in reality, a reef of sharp coral. And José and his men were not alone. Other landing boats had run into the same obstacle, their boats hopelessly lodged.

"We'll have to wade ashore!" José said finally. "Everyone, get out of the boat!"

José jumped into a cold sea that came up to his neck. An instant after he entered the water he felt a terrible surge of pain. A jagged shard of coral had cut deeply into his leg. Instinctively, he bent down and became submerged in the cold salty water. The shard had impaled his right leg. Under water, he broke off a six-inch piece extending from his thigh, then resurfaced again, gasping and coughing. Damn my luck, he thought.

At an excruciatingly slow pace, José and his comrades tried to carefully pick their way through the treacherous coral, holding their rifles over their heads in an attempt to keep them dry. Too late, he realized the walkie-talkie strapped to his belt had been rendered useless by the salt water. The gunfire became more intense as they neared the shore, but they pushed ahead, finally reaching the beach.

At a little after 3:00 a.m. the phone rang in Castro's Havana apartment. He was awake and answered it himself. Informed of the attack underway, he quickly ordered troops and artillery to the Zapata area and the Bay of Pigs. He also gave the order for an air strike against the ships. As he hung up the phone, Castro wondered whether this attack was just a ploy to throw him off while the real invasion was yet to come at another location. After all, who in their right mind would stage a nighttime invasion at the Bay of Pigs? It made no sense.

José crouched on the beach and tossed his useless walkie-talkie into the sand. He sat momentarily and rolled up his pants to examine the gouge in his leg, a piece of coral still deeply embedded into it. He ripped a portion of his pant leg off and bound his leg in an effort to stanch the bleeding. When he tried to stand again, he fell forward. It was getting harder to put any weight on it. Meanwhile, gunfire was going off all around him.

In the darkness, he could make out the forms of some of the troops who had reached the beach and were gradually working their way inland. Many others, however, were being picked off in boats that had hung up in the coral or, as he had done, were slowly trying to wade through the coral to the shore. It was all taking too long, he thought, far too long.

Then he heard the planes. At first he rejoiced, thinking it was the promised air support at last. But instead, a Cuban air force bomber leveled off and aligned itself with the exiles' command ship. In disbelief, he watched the *Maropa* take a direct hit. There was a flash and a thundering explosion followed by another. More planes came swooping down over the bay, and José and his troops began to take a pounding.

The gradual light of dawn revealed a grim scene. The *Maropa*, as well as the supply ship *Houston*, had both been critically hit and were sinking some 80 yards off the shore. It was especially painful to see the *Houston* go down, for with it, José knew, went tons of ammunition, guns, food and medical supplies. But there was no time to mourn.

José turned his back on the sinking ships and joined in the battle as they pushed inland, but the question kept resonating in his mind: "Where are our planes? What happened to the planes?"

By noon, official news of the attack had reached Las Tunas and the rest of Cuba, as Castro took to the airwaves on the state-controlled television and radio networks in the late morning. He looked sternly at the cameras and announced that the country was under attack by mercenaries of the imperialist United States. He said that the revolutionary armies had engaged the enemy and were gloriously defending the motherland.

The Montoro family, absent the imprisoned Miguel, gathered around the radio and listened as Castro pounded on the podium while urging all Cubans to take up arms against the "mercenary" invaders.

Nydia turned off the radio, unable to listen to it anymore.

Since Miguel had been taken the day before, she had learned that he was being held at the public school in Las Tunas, along with other community leaders.  She had also heard that Fernando García had been arrested outside of town, but it was unclear where he had been taken.

Rumors were everywhere that morning.  Despite Castro's confident proclamations, other radio broadcasts reported that the exile army had successfully established a beachhead. There was also talk of defections from the ranks of Castro's army, militia uprisings, and mutinies.

It did not escape Nydia's attention that Señora Manuel, along with various other members of the Committee for the Defense of the Revolution, had quietly taken down the signs posted on the doorways of their homes that indicated their positions of power.  On the outside chance the exile army was successful, they were choosing to become invisible.  How quickly their allegiance fades, she thought and shook her head in disgust.

The official news that President Kennedy had called off additional air strikes that were to occur on April 17 and 18 never reached José García.  In the wake of the political fallout from the poorly disguised planes and Cuba's accurate accusations in the United Nations, not to mention a terse note from Premier Khrushchev warning of Soviet involvement if Cuba were threatened, the White House folded its cards. Kennedy decided he did not wish to play this particular poker game anymore.

Pinned down on the beach with some 1,500 other soldiers and desperately waiting for reinforcements and the promised air support, a cold dark feeling crept into José's heart. It was becoming increasingly evident that he and his men had been abandoned. They were being pounded by Castro's now reinforced ground troops and his air force flew above them dropping bombs with impunity. All this, while their own ships and supplies lay sunken in the bay. Soon they would be surrounded; the only exits left being the Zapata Swamp or the sea, neither of which left much hope.

Without their walkie-talkies, José and his men were effectively cut off from any communication with the rest of the force, but it hardly mattered. It was clear to José that the mission was failing. Five of his men were dead and three others wounded, one critically. José did not count himself among the wounded, although he now had to use his rifle as a crutch in order to walk at all. They could no longer move forward, nor could they go back. José knew they were rapidly running out of options.

They did not surrender, but grimly fought on through the next day. The tattered force fought until they ran out of bullets, then followed José as he tried to lead an ill-advised retreat into the swamp. They never made it. Four more were killed before they were finally surrounded. With a rifle in the fixed-bayonet position inches from his throat, José García become one of 1,189 survivors captured that day.

In the early morning hours of April 20, Fidel Castro issued a victory statement. "The enemy of mercenaries has been totally crushed," he said perfunctorily. "The evil imperialist army has been defeated and repelled from the motherland. The so-called invincible forces of the United States has been overwhelmed by loyal Cuban troops." He had delivered the message in a stern and somber voice. Only after he stepped away from the cameras and lights, did he quietly smile and light a cigar. Class is dismissed, thought the Maximum Teacher; the lesson has been administered. His Soviet colleagues in Moscow would be very pleased to hear all the details.

José fully expected to be executed upon his capture, and he was more than ready for it. His sense of betrayal was complete. His men were dead, wounded or captured. The air support never materialized. Reinforcements never arrived. The invasion had become a fiasco more than a battle. But questions still rang in his ears... Why did they abandon us? Why were we left to die? What the hell had happened?

He began to feel more and more woozy, and his thought

process became increasingly less clear as he continued to lose blood from the deep cut on his leg. By the time Castro's troops shackled his legs and arms, he could barely stand and had to be lifted onto one of the trucks. He was only semi-conscious by the time the convoy arrived in Havana, where Castro would use the opportunity to display the captured troops to the public, branding them traitors, captured worms.

A mass trial would be held in the coming weeks and each captured freedom fighter would be sentenced to 30 years in prison. José, however, would not be among those tried. He died in his cell two days later due to his infected and untreated wound and, perhaps more so, because he simply gave up. He had the will to fight the battle, but not to live on through this humiliation.

Fernando was taken to Havana where he was accused and convicted of participating in covert operations with the intention of overthrowing the rightful government of Cuba and assisting in the exile invasion. He too, was sentenced to 30 years in prison, a term effectively stretching out beyond his anticipated life span. Upon learning the fate of his son two days into his own trial, he put his head in his shaking hands and wept openly.

As quickly as they had come down, the signs proclaiming residences as those inhabited by members of the Committee for the Defense of the Revolution were prominently displayed once again in their former locations. No one admitted or mentioned their removal. Life in Las Tunas returned to a strange kind of normalcy, but one in which it all seemed much, much worse.

Three days after the failed invasion ended, most of those citizens who had been detained were freed and allowed to return to their families. Nydia remembered waiting outside the school with Maria and her brothers when the guards released the detainees. One by one they came out, but Miguel did not appear.

"Where is my husband, Miguel Montoro?" she finally confronted one of the guards. After some discussion, one of them came back to her with the pronouncement, "Your husband has been taken to the police station for further questioning."

Nydia's heart sank. "When will he be released?" she asked, growing increasingly worried. "Why do you hold him?" she almost shouted.

The guard responded saying, "You may check on his status tomorrow," and he abruptly returned to his comrades and ignored her. Nydia was angry enough to spit in his face, but did not. Instead, she went home, but returned the next day, and the next, always to receive the same response.

On the third morning, Nydia knew what she had to do. She went to their bedroom dresser and from the bottom drawer took an envelope. She stared at it for some time before finally placing it into her purse and quickly walking down to the police station again.

When the guard appeared at the door, she handed the envelope to him. It contained all the money they had left, including that which Miguel had intended to use for their exit visas and to start their new life in America. The guard looked at it, then turned and left without comment.

Nydia waited and prayed. Within the hour, two guards ushered Miguel to the front door of the police station and roughly shoved him out. He stumbled, but did not fall. His eyes were sunken and his face looked drawn and hollow. Nydia ran to him.

"What have they done to you?" she said and then cried and hugged him, "What have they done?"

Miguel squinted in the bright light, holding his hands over his eyes to shade them. "I am fine, really," he said. Then he quietly asked her a one-word question, "Fernando?" Nydia shook her head no as she held him. "I am sorry to hear this," he said, shaking his head sadly.

"Let us go home," said Nydia.

When they reached the street, Maria and her brothers quickly converged on Miguel, and the family embraced in tears of gratitude that he was with them again. Then, they slowly walked down the street together, not talking; but each holding on to the others as if they were all they had left.

The large over-stuffed envelope, arriving as it did so many months later, initially confused Miguel. He had come home from another long day laboring at the plantation and found it waiting for him on the kitchen table.

"It came today," said Nydia, looking over her shoulder as she did the best she could with the sparse ingredients on hand to prepare dinner for the family.

He sat down wearily and studied the package. It indeed had his name on it, typewritten. But here was no return address and the postmark was from Mexico City, a place he had never visited nor did he know anyone living there. Suspiciously, he turned it over in his hands several times before finally opening it.

Inside were two smaller envelopes. One of them had his name written on it. He opened it first, and found a one page hand-written letter.

Dear Miguel,

I am writing this as you return home to Victoria de Las Tunas this evening after we have talked. You should know that I am still very encouraged and optimistic about our upcoming victory against the despicable Castro regime. But I am also a businessman and a realist. These skills have taught me to be prudent, and to try to ensure those who would help me are taken care of, as best I am able. I will soon visit you and ask for your help in our cause, and you will no doubt say yes.

I am preparing this package tonight and will send it to trusted friends in Mexico City with instructions to make the necessary arrangements in case we cannot celebrate our victory in Havana. If you receive this letter and its accompanying contents, obviously things have not gone as we had hoped.

As you read this, I am no doubt either dead or in prison. I hope the former is true, for I am too old a man to spend the rest of my days behind Castro's bars. In any case, you came to me to ask a favor and, instead, I asked for one from you. I hope no harm has come to you or your family as a result.

Miguel, you will always be a great friend to me and to Cuba, but it is now time to go.

Yours in friendship,
Fernando

The words blurred before Miguel. His eyes filled with tears. Nydia came and put her hands on his shoulders.

When he could speak, he called his children into the kitchen and read the letter aloud to the whole family. Then he opened the second envelope. It contained $2,000 in one-hundred-dollar American bills with a brief note in Fernando's handwriting which said, "Not enough to live on, but enough to start."

Miguel stood and said, "We will say a prayer for our friend, Fernando García, and then we will start to make arrangements. It is time to leave Cuba."

Nydia looked out the window of the plane again and saw this time only deep blue waters beneath them. The shimmering waves sparkled in the sun for as far as she could see. She realized she had been crying again. Quietly, she wiped her tears and said a final prayer for Fernando García.

# Chapter Four

Alberto crouched under his desk making monkey faces at Danny. They were supposed to have placed their heads between their knees with their backs to the windows as Miss McCory lead them in another "duck and cover" exercise. Danny's stomach actually hurt because he was trying so hard to hold in his laughter.

"Once again, let's all remember," said Miss McCory, "that in the event of actual nuclear attack, we should never look at the flash." She smiled patiently.

In the spring of 1962 at Parkwood Elementary School, "duck and cover" drills were like a game, and made for an amusing interlude between the regular class activities. Later, during recess, Danny punched Alberto squarely in the shoulder in retribution for his monkey faces. It was the kind of gesture shared between the best of young friends.

Alberto Pascual had arrived in Miami the year before as a *Pedro Pan*, one of some 14,000 young Cubans brought into the United States in the course of twenty-two months as part of an humanitarian effort sponsored through an unlikely combination of church and government resources. Like the other young immigrants, he arrived in Miami alone and bewildered. He was initially placed in a camp with hundreds of other young Cuban boys and girls while his parents, desperately poor, remained behind in a Havana ghetto.

Now Alberto ran across the playground, with Danny in hot pursuit, and he climbed to the top of the monkey bars. He didn't have Danny's athletic build, but he was quick and always moved with a certain grace. He was also stronger than he looked. His sinewy frame carried all muscle and no fat. As Danny and Alberto perched themselves on top of the monkey bars, the notion of a real nuclear attack was so far beyond their comprehension as to be impossible.

Life was almost making sense to Alberto again, a year since he had been "adopted" by George and Mary Kendall, a childless couple who lived down the street from Danny Reynolds' family. The Kendall's were a quiet and devout Christian couple who considered it an act of their faith to provide a safe and nurturing home for Alberto until such time as he could be reunited with his family.

Danny and Alberto had quickly fallen in together despite the fact that Alberto arrived knowing almost no English. He learned quickly, finding that at eight years old, a second language is an easy thing to acquire. Within a few months, Alberto had adjusted remarkably well to his new life. He still had his occasional dark moments and still missed his "real" family, but his cheerful and optimistic nature usually overcame any despair.

Halfway around the world, on a continent known to Danny and Alberto, or any of their classmates, only as a place on a map, an event was unfolding that would soon affect their lives. That April U.S. Jupiter missiles became operational in Turkey and the nuclear balance of the world shifted markedly. The newly installed missile batteries would have the ability to reach Moscow within minutes.

The ramifications of this development were not missed by Soviet Premier Nikita Khrushchev. The news reached him while he was vacationing on the Black Sea. Infuriated, he cut short his holiday and returned to Moscow, where he hastily gathered his closest advisors at the Kremlin. The subject of the meeting was how best to respond to this dangerous new American threat at their doorstep. It was clear to Khrushchev that this latest development gave the Americans a clear offensive advantage in the ongoing nuclear chess game they were playing. Moscow could be in ashes before a single missile could be launched in return. Khrushchev considered it audacious of the young new American president to think he could do this without a response.

In the course of the meeting, the possibility of deploying similar missiles in Cuba was brought up. It was an interesting notion, he thought, and could be considered a "tit for tat" sort of arrangement. If the Americans could have missiles only hundreds of miles from the Kremlin, why should *we* not be allowed to have them off the Florida coast? From Cuba, an ICBM could easily reach Washington or New York. Khrushchev smiled as the afternoon discussions wore on. He thought about the rash American president feeling the hot breath of the USSR on his neck for a change.

The only inherent risk, Khrushchev knew, was Castro. He was young, still a wild-eyed revolutionary in many ways, and immature in matters of this nature. He would have to be handled, thought Khrushchev.

There were more meetings but by May, a detailed plan had been developed on Khrushchev's orders, and a high-level delegation was sent to Cuba to secretly meet with Fidel Castro and his brother Raúl, the Minister of Defense. The Maximum Leader greeted them cordially and listened to the proposal with unusually few interjections.

Castro's elation over the Bay of Pigs victory was not long lived. He was still faced with the real and growing threat of a full-fledged American invasion of his country; this in addition to an array of covert activities orchestrated by the despicable Kennedy brothers. Their outrageous acts had ranged from sabotage and intelligence actions, to the development of underground revolutionary groups within Cuba, to assassination attempts on his life.

He had also nervously watched increasingly larger and more frequent U.S. military exercises conducted in the Caribbean throughout the past year. Castro was almost certain it was a pretext to a full-scale invasion of his country.

The timing of this opportunity could not be better, thought Castro. It would be an arrangement of convenience for both the Soviet Union and Cuba, one that would serve them well in combating the aggressive tendencies of the imperialistic American State. From the Soviet perspective, Castro saw it would bring the "nuclear balance" back to a more central position, not to mention deterring Kennedy's strong wish to invade Cuba.

Most importantly, though, it would give the Maximum Leader the ability to strike fear into the heart of America, a country that recklessly rattled its sabers while feeling impervious to danger. All this would change now. The Maximum Leader would be a player in the Big Game. His influence would be felt, even in the White House.

Castro deferred from committing to an agreement that night, insisting that he must talk with his closest advisors. It was an attempt on his part not to seem overly enthusiastic. That night in the Presidential Palace, Castro and his comrades smoked cigars and toasted this great windfall with cognac. The next morning, he quickly agreed to accept the deployment of Soviet nuclear missiles and forces in Cuba.

Additional meetings were held in Havana and Moscow over the course of the next weeks and months to finalize the details. Ultimately, it was agreed that 24 medium-range ballistic missile launchers, as well as 16 intermediate-range launchers, each equipped with two missiles and a warhead, would be shipped to Cuba. They would be accompanied by SA-2 surface-to-air missile batteries, MiG-21 interceptors, IL-28 bombers, and Komar-class missile boats. It amounted to a huge military buildup in Cuba.

Beginning in early summer and stretching through the fall, Soviet cargo ships began sailing from the Baltic and Black Seas to Cuba with their cloaked cargo holds filled.

On an evening late that August, Danny and Alberto perched comfortably in the towering old oak tree in Danny's backyard.

It was their favorite place, their hideout, their retreat. The summer was over and another school year was now just a week away from beginning. On this night, as many others, they leaned back on their respective branches and talked while watching the stars.

"Tell me about life again, you know, before you came here. I like your stories," said Danny.

"What do you want to know, amigo? I was very young and do not remember everything."

"I dunno. Did you listen to music?"

"I will tell you a story about the music," said Alberto. "My father once knew a man who played music. He was not from Havana, but sometimes he would travel there. I do not know where he lived, but he traveled much and played his guitar in many places. They said he could make a guitar cry."

Danny laughed. "You mean the *way* he played the guitar could make somebody cry! You're doing your crazy English again!"

"I am not crazy with my English. He could make his guitar cry. I swear this to you. When he would play it, they said it sounded like a woman who is singing very sadly like she is crying. This is true. I do not make this up."

"It sounded like a woman crying? Really?"

"Yes, it was very sad, very beautiful."

"Did you ever hear it?" asked Danny.

"No, my father only told me of this man. I was too young. I do not remember."

"Do you think he ever played happy songs?"

"Of course, many happy songs; but that is another thing," said Alberto.

There was silence between them for a while.

"Tell me about your family, your *real* family," said Danny.

"Well," said Alberto stretching, "to begin with, my sister is beautiful. She is the most beautiful girl in the world. And I mean to say nothing unkind about anyone in your family by this. My mother, she is a saint, and my father is honest and brave, and he knows much of the sea. That is my family."

"I know, I know," said Danny rolling his eyes. "You've already told me that a million times. Tell me something else about them, something new."

"They are very poor, but this I have also told you before. There were many times I remember that we did not eat because there was no food. And this made my mother cry but she would try to hide it from my father, because it made him angry."

"He got angry at your mom?"

"No, no. He was angry because there was no food and we were all hungry. There are many people in Havana who are hungry. Some of them steal, but my father would not allow this. He would not allow us to beg or to steal. Never."

"So, what did you eat?"

"My father is a fisherman. This makes him very little money. Sometimes there are no fish and there is nothing that can be done. But when he finds the fish, he always catches them because he understands them and he talks to them."

"He talks to them? Oh brother."

"Of course. The best fisherman knows what to say to the fishes so they will come to him. If he is very good, they will jump into his net because he has asked them to and because they know he is such a good fisherman."

"I dunno Alberto, all this stuff about crying guitars and fish that talk. I think you're crazy."

"No, no, the fish do not talk. Don't be silly. Fish cannot talk. There is no such thing. The fisherman talks *to* the fish. This is how it is done. The fish only listen. And a very good fisherman can talk and make the fish understand what he wishes them to do. My father is such a fisherman. This is the truth. I swear it."

"I bet you ate a lot of fish, huh?"

"My mother can cook any kind of fish in the ocean. She is the best fish cook in all of Havana."

"She is?"

"Yes, you do not believe me?"

"Sure, Alberto, I believe you." Danny stretched and thought for a moment. "When you first got here, were you scared?" he asked.

Alberto nodded. "Yes, I am very scared. No, I *was* very scared. My mother and father could not take me to the airport in Havana because they were afraid they might be arrested. Instead, Father Cabrera took me. He gave me a piece of paper with a name on it. He said someone would be waiting for me at the airport in Miami.

"Before I left, my father gave me a twenty-dollar American bill. He showed me how to put it under the lining of my shoe, so if a guard checked, he would not find it. I think my father saved a long time to have that much money. In Havana, twenty American dollars is very, very much money.

"When we got to the airport in Havana, Father Cabrera was very worried they would stop us and not allow me to get on the plane. I had only the clothes I wore. The guards still searched me, but they did not look in my shoe," he added smiling.

"What happened when you got to Miami?"

Alberto paused and finally said, "Nothing at first. I sat on a bench. I was alone and I could not ask anyone for help because I could not speak English. After a long time an old man came up to me. He was not a priest, but he seemed like a priest. I think he was an angel, maybe an archangel. You know, archangels are the strongest. Do you believe in angels, amigo?"

"Sure, I guess," shrugged Danny.

"This old man, who was an archangel, he came down from Heaven to help me."

"Why do you think he was an archangel? Maybe it was a priest or somebody."

"No, he spoke Spanish to me before he knew I could not speak English. But he did not speak the Spanish of Havana. He was from somewhere else, maybe Santiago. He did not know my name, and when I showed the piece of paper Father Cabrera gave me, he only shrugged his shoulders and smiled. But he knew where I needed to go. He took me to the Processing Center, and when I turned to thank him, he was gone. They wanted to know how I got there, and I told them an old man brought me there, but they knew of no such man."

"Wow, he was just gone?"

"Yes," said Alberto. "I think he went back to Heaven."

They both paused and thought about that for a while before Danny asked, "What was it like at the Processing Center?"

"It was like a big school, except you slept there, too. There were beds and there was food, but all the beds were in one big room, so it was hard to sleep at first."

"I bet you were happy when you got to go home with the Kendalls."

"Yes, I am happy, but I still miss my real family. Every night I pray that they are okay and safe and that they have found some food to eat. Someday I will return to Cuba and get my family and bring them here. This I promise you."

"I'll help you," said Danny, "I will."

"Good. Maybe the archangel will help again, too," said Alberto, "But don't tell anyone. It will be our secret mission."

They stayed in the tree talking until Mrs. Kendall called for Alberto and soon after, Danny's mom called for him.

A thousand miles away from Miami and Danny's backyard, the results of another secret mission were being relayed to President Kennedy in the Oval Office. A U-2 spy plane flying over Cuba on August 29 had photographed Soviet SA-2 surface-to-air missiles and coastal defense cruise missiles already deployed. Kennedy was enraged at this discovery and insisted that his staff immediately draft a release stating "the gravest issues would arise" if the presence of offensive ground-to-ground missiles or other significant offensive capabilities were found in Cuba.

Unknown to Kennedy, the photographs failed to reveal evidence of construction around San Cristóbal, Cuba, where the first nuclear missile sites would be built. Within a week, increasing numbers of elite Soviet troops began arriving in Cuba. In mid-September, a Soviet cargo ship called the *Poltava* arrived in Mariel with the first shipment of medium-range ballistic missiles. Undetected by the U.S. surveillance, they were unloaded and taken by truck to San Cristóbal.

It was a Monday evening, October 22. The Reynolds family, including Danny, sat in front of their television set in stunned silence as the President of the United States announced that offensive missile sites were being built in Cuba. Kennedy stated his intention to meet the threat through a "strict quarantine," in effect a blockade of the island, and heightened military buildup within the United States.

Staring grimly at the camera, Kennedy announced that a missile attack launched from Cuba against the United States would be considered as an attack by the Soviet Union "requiring a full retaliatory response."

"My God," said Danny's father, "this could be World War Three," and instantly regretted saying it aloud. He turned toward his son, but Danny was already out the door, running as hard and fast as he could toward the Kendall's house down the street. He pounded on the door of the bungalow until Mr. Kendall opened it.

"Oh, Danny, come in. We were just watching the television," he said with a serious tone.

"Can I see Alberto, please?" asked Danny, still breathing hard.

Then Danny saw his friend quietly sitting on the couch in the living room. Tears were running down his cheeks. He went over to sit beside him. Instinctively, Danny offered Alberto a stick of gum that he silently took, and together they listened to Kennedy finish his speech on the small black and white screen in the Kendall's living room.

"I want to say a few words to the captive people of Cuba, to whom this speech is being directly carried by special radio facilities," said Kennedy. "Most Cubans," he said, "look forward to the time when they will be truly free..." He went on to claim that Castro had betrayed the Cuban people by turning their country into a Soviet base. He urged them to throw Castro out.

In truth, Kennedy had known about the offensive missiles for several days before his speech. A U-2 flight on October 14 had finally produced photographs of the missile site at San Cristóbal, but Kennedy wanted to keep his knowledge of it secret until the administration had formulated a response plan. Despite their attempts at secrecy, however, several newspapers, including the *New York Times* and *Washington Post*, had pieced together the story. It took phone calls directly to the publishers from both Kennedy and Robert McNamara to coerce the papers into holding the stories until after Kennedy's speech.

U.S. military forces worldwide were immediately placed on heightened alert, including missile crews and Polaris nuclear submarines. Even before Kennedy finished addressing the nation, interceptor aircraft were flying over the skies of south Florida, just in case Cuba should react on its own.

On the morning of Wednesday, October 24, 1962, the U.S. Strategic Air Command moved its alert status to DEFCON 2. For the first time in history, the nation was one step away from an actual nuclear engagement.

"Do you think your family knows what's going on?" asked Danny when the President's address had ended.

"I don't know," Alberto said. "They have no television or radio."

In fact, the vast majority of Cuban citizens, including Alberto's parents, did not even know there was a missile crisis. Castro revealed nothing to the Cuban public, closely keeping all information within his tight inner circle.

In the United States, though, the news permeated the airwaves and the newspapers. This was especially the case in south Florida. Over the course of the next two weeks, hundreds of thousands of troops would flood into the southernmost state. Long trains carrying missiles and tanks ran 24 hours a day, always working their way south. Homestead Air Force Base was reactivated and troops took over old packing plants while tents were set up in tomato fields. Around Miami, missile batteries were quickly established, and camouflaged vehicles and artillery headed south on Route U.S. 1 to install other missile units in the Florida Keys. Naval destroyers patrolled off the Florida coast.

The next morning, the *Miami Herald* ran a front-page map indicating the results if the two most likely targets, Miami's international airport and the Homestead Air Force Base, were hit with nuclear missiles. The neighborhood where Danny and Alberto lived was squarely within the overlapping circles of destruction.

Military jets flew overhead night and day and air raid sirens were tested throughout the city at all hours. There were many neighbors who chose to leave, packing up their families, and heading north, but the Reynolds and Kendall families remained. Their television sets were constantly on as news reports and coverage of proceedings at the United Nations droned on.

Danny and Alberto continued to attend school, but were distracted by the events around them. The daily "duck and cover" drills, however, took on a grim reality. Like the other students, they brought bottled water, canned food and blankets to school as requested, as if that would somehow help in the event of a nuclear exchange.

In the exile community of Miami, there were grave worries about family members and friends still remaining in Cuba. Overwhelmingly patriotic, the Cubans living in the U.S. rallied behind the President and the U.S. government, although there were still deep emotional scars from the Bay of Pigs disaster. Many of the men who fought and were captured as part of Brigade 2506 remained imprisoned in Cuba.

Except for the Batistianos, many of whom managed to leave with money and possessions, most of the exile community lived in poverty, having arrived with very little. In a small coffee shop in the district that would one day become known as "Little Havana," a young Cuban girl named Elena listened to her father talking with a customer.

"This whole awful thing could have been prevented if Kennedy had done what he needed to do last year," he said. "If the Bay of Pigs invasion had succeeded, there would be no more of Castro's lies and there would be no missiles in Cuba."

Sometime after midnight on Saturday, October 27, at the height of the tension, Fidel Castro dictated an urgent letter to Khrushchev from the Soviet embassy in Havana, making use of its communication facilities as well as its bomb shelter. He was certain that a U.S. invasion was imminent, probably in the form of a massive air raid before an actual landing. Fearing such an attack, he urged Khrushchev to authorize a preemptive strike against the United States. His words would shock even Khrushchev.

"That would be the moment," Castro wrote, "to eliminate such danger forever through an act of clear legitimate self defense, however harsh and terrible the solution would be, for there is no other." He had the message sent at the highest priority to Khrushchev's attention.

Around noon the next day a U-2 plane was shot down over

Cuba by a SAM missile battery under Soviet control and its pilot was killed. Later that afternoon, six U.S. low-level reconnaissance planes flew over the missile sites at San Cristóbal and Sagua la Grande. Castro ordered Cuban anti-aircraft sites to fire on any U.S. reconnaissance flights, and they did. One plane was hit, but managed to return safely to the U.S. mainland.

Khrushchev, however, was already secretly negotiating with Kennedy to arrive at a settlement. The nuclear abyss had opened too quickly, and Castro's note only made him more anxious to settle the situation and keep it from spinning completely out of control. The Soviets would remove the missiles in exchange for a public U.S. promise not to invade Cuba and a private promise to remove the newly installed missiles in Turkey.

He decided he would inform Castro only after the deal had been made.

On the evening of October 28, Castro was alone in his large ornate office within the Presidential Palace. He had been sitting motionless behind his desk for some time. Then he picked up the heavy ashtray on his desk and flung it against the far wall where it shattered. A guard quickly appeared in the doorway, but Castro shouted for him to return to his post.

He turned away from his desk and walked out the doorway to the balcony overlooking the Revolutionary Plaza where he had addressed so many cheering crowds. On his desk was the letter from Khrushchev informing him that an agreement had been made with the United States and outlining the terms which with he would have to live.

The missile crisis was over. Castro would lose his Soviet missiles and his bombers and the nuclear edge he had so yearned to have. The fear he wished to project into the heart of imperialistic America could no longer be launched from Cuban soil.

Worse, this deal had been struck without his involvement or knowledge. In the end, neither he nor his new communist Cuba had been considered crucial on the world stage, by Khrushchev or Kennedy. In a silent rage, he stood on the balcony with his fists clenched and tried to deal with a humiliation his ego could not bear.

"Hey, Alberto," said Danny in the darkness of their pup tent. They were camping in the backyard. "Are you still awake?"

"Sure, amigo," said Alberto. "I'm awake." He rolled over in his sleeping bag and stretched.

"What do you think would have happened, you know, if the Russians hadn't backed down in Cuba?"

"I'm not sure. I guess it could have been pretty bad."

"Yeah. You know, that was the first time I ever saw my dad scared," said Danny.

"There's nothing wrong with being scared," said Alberto. "I think you can be brave and be scared at the same time. It's what you do after you're scared that counts."

"Yeah, I guess so," said Danny. He nestled back down in the sleeping bag. Neither one said anything else and eventually the sound of their slowed breathing was lost in the chatter of cicadas.

# Chapter
# Five

I t was three days before Christmas and Miami's International Airport was bustling with holiday travelers. The Kendall's blue Buick station wagon proceeded up the ramp to the drop-off area under the cantilevered overhang. The Kendalls sat up front, Danny's parents in the back seat with Danny, and Alberto sat cross-legged in the luggage area at the rear of the car.

"We appreciate the lift," said Danny's father, "See you in a couple weeks."

"Have a wonderful trip to Mexico!" said Mrs. Kendall. "Be sure to send us a postcard!"

Alberto grinned at Danny as the rear door swung open and they climbed out. "I'll see you in a couple weeks, amigo," he said.

"I wish you were coming, too," said Danny.

They waved as the Kendalls and Alberto pulled away, then carried their luggage into the terminal. With the increased holiday travelers, the lobby was even more crowded than usual. Danny noticed a large crowd clustered around one of the arrival gates. There were reporters and also some news camera crews. Flashbulbs were going off in a frenzy.

"It's the new arrivals from Cuba," Mr. Reynolds said as they walked toward the crowd. "Since they started the Freedom Flights again, there's been a steady flow of immigrants. Sometimes I wonder if there's going to be anybody left over there except Castro by the time they get done."

As they passed by, they were close enough to hear some of the reporters shouting questions to the newly arrived Cuban immigrants.

"How does it feel to be in America?"

"What do you think about the Castro regime?"

"Does anybody speak English? I need to get a few quotes."

Then Danny saw her. She was a young girl in a white dress. Her dark hair came to her shoulders and she wore a white bow in it. Her brown eyes seemed to take in everything around her with a sense of awe. She was standing next to a middle-aged couple, perhaps her father and mother. Two older boys stood beside her.

There was something about her that Danny could not describe, but he felt himself drawn to her. She looked interested by all the attention and confusion, but not afraid. That was what struck him the most.

She finally noticed him and Danny realized he was smiling at her involuntarily. In those seconds he was thinking about Alberto, how lonely and scared he must have been when he arrived in America. He remembered how much it had meant to Alberto that somebody had been kind to him. Whether it was an archangel or not, it had made all the difference.

Danny dug deep into his jeans pocket and found his pack of Wrigley's gum. Just as they passed each other, he paused and offered her a stick. His heart was pounding like he'd just run a mile at top speed. Her eyes grew bigger. She looked down at his hands, and then she looked into his eyes.

Maria squinted as she entered the terminal and flash bulbs went off around her. There were so many people, everyone was speaking English, and some people were shouting questions that she could not understand. So this, she thought, is America!

At first she did not notice the young boy looking at her. Then he smiled. Why would anyone in this country of strangers be smiling at her? She did not recognize him but she was sure he was staring directly at her. She looked at his tousled hair and his blue eyes and for just a moment, he seemed somehow familiar to her, but that would be impossible. She shrugged off a shiver and stepped closer to her father.

Now he approached as if to talk to her, and her heart skipped a beat, because she knew only a few words of English. Suddenly he stopped right in front of her. He dug into his pockets and now opened his hand to her. He was offering something to her. Their faces were very close. She looked down and saw the stick of gum. At first she didn't know what it was, but she took it quietly saying, "Gracias," and smiled directly into his eyes.

The flash of another camera illuminated the scene, and for an instant, Maria and Danny were frozen in time, each smiling at each other with a stick of gum between them.

"Thanks kids. Nice shot," said the photographer from the *Miami Herald*. "That's what I call international diplomacy," he mused to himself as he followed the crowd and continued to snap photos.

"Danny, let's go, son," called his father from where the rest of his family stood waiting across the crowded terminal. Danny nodded, but turned to Maria one more time, even though she was now several steps away as her father gently tugged her along. She glanced back for a moment and held her hand up in a small wave to him before she and her family were engulfed in the crowd.

Danny stood there feeling slightly light-headed. His heart was still beating quickly and he felt the butterflies swirling in his stomach. It was not an unpleasant feeling, just one he'd never known before. There was something about that girl, he knew, but could not quite understand what. It was as if he'd just passed through the tail of a comet. Everything was brighter around him, almost shimmering.

Maybe that's what it's like to meet an angel, he thought, then ran to catch up with his family.

# Chapter
# Six

"Hurry up, Maria or we'll be late!" shouted Elena from downstairs.

"Yes, yes, I'm coming! I'll be right there," Maria promised, as she looked at herself in the dresser mirror one last time. The reflection was of a beautiful young woman with shoulder-length dark hair and brown eyes in a demure, but elegant, black party dress. Now in her junior year at the University of Miami, Maria was celebrating her 21$^{st}$ birthday this evening.

Much had changed in the 11 years since the Montoro's arrival in Miami, when the prospects of making a life for themselves in this new country seemed so grim. It had been a struggle, but they had made the best of it and had dedicated themselves to doing what had to be done to survive and to get ahead.

The biggest initial hurdle was the language barrier. It was easiest for Maria and her brothers. The children were quick to pick up words and phrases in English at school and on the playground. It was perhaps hardest on her father; Miguel would always feel more comfortable expressing himself in his native Spanish.

To help support the family, Maria's mother, like many other Cuban wives, sought work in a Hialeah garment factory where the wages were low, the work was hard, and the hours were long. Importantly, though, it provided the money the family needed to survive in those initial months. Having quickly learned the trade, Nydia managed to save enough money to buy her own sewing machine, and soon she was doing work on her own.

Miguel faced a more difficult struggle to establish his own business. The money from Fernando had only been enough to get the Montoros settled in a one-bedroom apartment. The established banking institutions of that day were reluctant to lend money to fresh immigrants arriving from Cuba. To start a business meant financing it with meager personal savings or whatever small amounts of borrowed funds could be raised from family and friends.

Miguel started by studying English every day and, in the evenings, Maria and the boys would help him practice. He also investigated some of the sugar cane plantations in south Florida and talked to those who worked at them. He devised a business plan to provide supplies and eventually perhaps equipment to these firms. Armed with his business plan and dressed in his only suit, he ventured down to the local branch of one of the major Miami banks.

He arrived early for his appointment and patiently waited 20 minutes after his scheduled time before asking the receptionist when he might be seen. She merely shrugged and went back to her typing. Finally, the door of the office opened and an overweight man in his 50s appeared, wearing thick black-framed glasses with red suspenders that strained to hold up wrinkled gray trousers. Perspiration stains blemished the armpits of his white shirt as he put his hand on the shoulder of the well-dressed middle-aged gentleman with whom he had just finished speaking.

"Glad to be of help, Frank," he said with feigned joviality as he glanced down at his watch. He rolled his eyes at the receptionist when he saw Miguel waiting, but waved him in anyway. Harry Curtis sighed as he closed the door, wondering when he was finally going to be able to get some lunch.

In his best English, Miguel presented his business plan and the basis for needing a loan. He explained that he would like to start a company selling supplies and fertilizer to the sugar plantations in southern Florida.

"I have run a plantation in Cuba," said Miguel. "It was in our family for many years and I understand the business very well. It is not so different here in America than it was in Cuba."

Harry Curtis pushed back the glasses that chronically slid

down his nose and pretended to study Miguel's business plan. His stomach growled. These Cuban immigrants just don't get it, he thought. They don't understand how things are done. There was no way he would ever submit the paperwork for this kind of a loan with *his* signature attached to it.

"It's a collateral issue, you see, um, Mr. Montoro," he sighed. "You have no investment capital. You have no collateral to guarantee any kind of a loan. I realize the amount isn't very much, but you see we just don't do things that way in this country. We don't make loans at this bank without sufficient guarantees."

He smiled thinly, unsure how much Miguel had understood. "Mr. Montoro, let me be frank with you. We don't have anybody here who speaks Spanish. So if you're having trouble understanding what I'm saying to you, I'd suggest you come back with somebody who speaks English a little better maybe." He smiled again and closed the folder with finality, pushing it back across the desk at Miguel.

"I can speak English," said Miguel, now standing formally. "I understand what you have told me." He spoke slowly and purposely. "If I had such money, such capital, I would not ask for it in the first place. I have the necessary experience in this area. The business will be a success and I will repay you with interest. On this I can give you my word."

"Your *word?*" asked Harry, almost laughing out loud. "Mr. Montoro, I don't know how banking was done in Cuba before Castro came in, but we're not in the business of making unsecured loans based on anybody's word. Sorry."

In the end, Harry got his lunch, but lost a customer, and many others like him.

Slowly, however, the business climate in Miami changed. Despite the dominance of the established financial institutions, a few small neighborhood banks began to crop up, most created with Latin American capital. While their funds were very limited, their terms were quite flexible. Among the Cuban exiles, there were those who arrived with banking backgrounds. Many of them found employment in these upstart financial endeavors. Some of them even worked their way to management positions, and they looked much more favorably upon doing business with their Cuban compatriots than did the large established banks.

The attitude of the new small banks was to look at the character and integrity of the applicant instead of solely the balance sheet or business plan presented. Soon it became possible in the Cuban community to secure a small loan with little or no capital.

It was such a loan that Miguel eventually applied for and received. He had heard about the small bank that had opened in the neighborhood, but was initially reluctant to apply. He had already been turned down by several other American bankers like Harry Curtis.

Miguel again wore his one suit and presented the same business plan. This time there was no receptionist and no waiting. The small two-room office had only the barest of furnishings, but he was seen immediately by a Señor Felize. They began speaking English, but soon lapsed into Spanish.

Señor Felize explained that he had been a banker in Havana before fleeing to the U.S. He complimented Miguel on making the effort to prepare his business plan in English. "We need to master this language if we are to succeed here," he said.

Surprisingly, the subject of collateral never came up. "I understand you come from Las Tunas," he said. "I know of your family. I have also asked about you in this community, and all say you are an honorable man. What you ask for is a reasonable amount of money to start this business. If the interest rate and terms are acceptable to you, we have only to draw up the papers. I wish you every success in this endeavor."

Similar stories were played out again and again as the Cuban enclave in Miami grew in confidence and economic power. The large banking institutions eventually caught on and alarmed at their loss of business, made hurried attempts to hire Cubans, or at least Spanish-speaking managers, but it was too late. The invisible walls of the Cuban enclave had closed, and they were on the outside. Harry Curtis, and many others like him, found themselves out of clients and, ultimately, out of jobs.

Maria was just stepping into the hallway when she found Elena coming up the stairs.

"Well, it's about time," Elena said smiling.

Maria and Elena first met immediately after the Montoro family's arrival in Miami. The Montoro's first apartment was above a coffee shop that Elena's parents ran near Calle Ocho. A year older than Maria, Elena was in her last year at the University of Miami majoring in political science. It suited her well, as she lived and breathed politics.

Elena applied both her passion and her intellectual skills to delve into the complex social currents within the Cuban exile community where she lived. She knew that small banking institutions were able to have zero defaults on their loans because the loyalty and solidarity of the Cuban community demanded their prompt repayment. To not repay a loan would be to lose face and become an outcast within the community. She understood why Cuban workers would often join unions in established mainstream companies, but would never organize in a Cuban-owned firm. She also understood the fierce anti-Communist stance within a community that had initially cheered Castro, only to be betrayed by him and again later by Kennedy at the Bay of Pigs. She knew and understood the deep anger that still existed over the agreement between Kennedy and Khrushchev that put to an end any hopes of a U.S.-backed effort to retake the reins of government from Castro.

Elena understood these things on both an intellectual and an emotional level. She and Maria would discuss it for hours, often disagreeing. Of the two, Elena was more radical in her beliefs and outlook. She saw the anti-Castro cause as a fierce struggle that had to be won at all costs in order to rid Cuba of an oppressive regime. There could be no compromise. Maria, following her journalistic instincts, sought to understand the issues and ongoing conflict and still yearned for the possibility of a peaceful solution in her native land.

"You are a child if you make yourself believe such a thing is possible," said Elena.

"Sometimes it takes the child within us to see new possibilities," Maria responded.

Despite their differences, Maria and Elena were best of friends, and confidantes as well as foils. They arrived at the foot of the stairs in a flurry, laughing.

"Maria, you look so lovely," said her father as he turned, surprised. She kissed him on his cheek. "Thank you, Daddy.

Sorry I kept you waiting. Let's go," she said.

The whole Montoro family and Elena, who was considered a family member, dined that evening at one of Miami's best restaurants. Miguel, ever the proud father, sat at the head of the table with Nydia. Maria, her brothers, and Elena sat in the other seats as Miguel raised his glass in a toast.

"I have so much to be thankful for. I have been blessed with a wonderful family, a comfortable home, and a solid business—and all of this in a free country. I have also been blessed with a wonderful wife and children. And today, my beautiful and intelligent daughter turns twenty-one. She is all grown up, and I could not be more proud of her. Happy birthday, Maria." They all clapped.

After dinner, Maria danced with her father at his insistence. "It's a small favor for an old man," he whispered to her. Together, the father and daughter moved elegantly across the floor. When they finished, she sat down, flushed and happy, beside Elena.

"Tonight, I will take you out for a celebration cocktail," said Elena. "I want you to meet some friends."

"From the university?" asked Maria.

"Some yes, others no. They are all very interesting people, though. You bury yourself so much in your studies; you're like a hermit these days. Remember how we used to go out dancing all the time? We need to do more of that again."

When they arrived at a popular and upscale bar on the south side of Miami, the parking lot was filled so Elena handed the keys to the attendant outside. Inside it was crowded and loud with sounds of music and conversations. No sooner had they reached the bar, than a handsome young Cuban stepped forward and kissed Elena on the cheek, insisting on getting them drinks of their choice.

"Alberto," said Elena, "I would like you to meet my very good friend Maria. It's her birthday. Maria, this is Alberto Pascual. He is somewhat of a rogue, so watch out for him."

Alberto smiled warmly, kissed Maria's hand, and congratulated her. In moments he was back with their drinks. "I would also like to introduce you to someone," he said, "if I could just find him."

They chatted a few minutes before Dan stepped out of the crowd clustered around the bar and walked toward them. He looked lean and trim in his sport coat and casual slacks, and definitely not Cuban. Maria unconsciously raised her eyebrows as she watched him approach.

"This is who I was telling you about," said Alberto. "I would like you to meet my little brother, Dan Reynolds."

Maria looked confused while Alberto and Elena laughed heartily.

"Let's say Alberto and Dan sort of grew up together and are close enough to call each other brothers without the benefit of having the same parents," explained Elena.

"Yes, I figured as much," Maria said with a smile and then paused. "It's just that you look so familiar to me. It's as if I should know you, but I don't think I do."

Dan smiled back. "Well, perhaps you should," he said. "After all, I'm in your economics class. But it's a big lecture hall, and it's hard to remember all those faces."

Embarrassed, Maria said, "I'm sorry. I should have known. It *is* a crowded lecture hall," she agreed, adding, "I have to admit that economics is not my favorite subject. It takes all of my concentration just to understand some of that material."

Dan laughed and agreed. In truth, he had noticed Maria the first day of class and had the same feeling of déjà vu, like bumping into an old friend in unfamiliar surroundings and not being able to place them. In fact, every time the class met, he would look about the hall trying to spot her. He was attracted to her at once, and not just because of her beauty. There was something about her; he just couldn't place it. Perhaps that's why he never acted on it, he thought.

"So, tell me, how do you know each other?" Maria asked, looking at Elena and then Alberto.

"Oh, it's a long story," said Elena. "Alberto lives and works on his boat. He is quite the Cuban sea captain," she added, laughing. Maria noticed that while Alberto smiled and nodded, his eyes grew suddenly cooler, more reserved and serious.

"I'm just a simple boat captain," he said, "who sometimes gets others to pay him to take them fishing. That's all."

There was a moment of awkward silence before Dan suggested they share a booth and sit and talk for a while. Their conversation was casual and light. Dan and Alberto seemed to be each other's biggest fans as they alternately told funny stories and swapped punch lines. Maria laughed until her cheeks hurt and was about to suggest she and Elena should finally think about going home when she noticed Dan studying her closely.

"You make me a little nervous," she said, "when you stare at me like that for more than two minutes or so."

"Oh, I'm sorry. I didn't mean to. It's just, I feel like I know you from somewhere, and not from class. I just can't figure out when and where. That sounds like a line, but believe me, it's not," he added.

"Okay," she said and smiled, "I believe you."

After they finished their drinks, Elena and Maria said their good-byes to Dan and Alberto with the promise to get together again as a group soon.

In the car on their way home, Maria said, "Well, tell me about this Alberto. How long have you known him, and why have I never heard you mention him before?"

"It's not romantic with Alberto. He is quite active in the exile cause," she said purposely being vague. "We've gone out before, but Alberto has many girlfriends. He never seems to let anyone get too close. Did you know he was a Pedro Pan? He came over at about the same age as you, but all alone."

"What about his family?" asked Maria.

"Still in Cuba, I'm afraid." Elena paused. "So, what do you think about this guy Dan? Am I blind, or did I see you almost swoon when you first saw him?"

Maria laughed. "There *is* something about him," she said. "I'm just not sure what it is yet. Had you met him before?"

"No, tonight was the first time. Alberto has mentioned him before, though. They've been best friends forever, just like us," she said smiling. "He certainly was looking at you tonight," she added.

"I know," said Maria. "I know."

Maria spent the summer between her junior and senior years working as an intern at the *Miami Herald*. As she had hoped, it led to a full-time position when the *Herald* made her an offer to report on Latin American affairs just before her graduation.

"Well, congratulations!" said Elena on the phone when she heard the news. "So you're really going to become a hotshot reporter for that Anglo newspaper!" she added only half joking. Elena had encouraged Maria to work for one of the smaller Spanish-language publications in the Miami area, but Maria wanted the experience that could be found only on a major daily newspaper.

The past year had been busy for both of them, leaving little time for socializing. Elena had started organizing informal weekly gatherings, sometimes at her dormitory other times in various coffee shops, to discuss what was happening within the Latino population, both in Cuba and in the exile community of Miami.

Initially, it was mostly attended by university students and professors, but the meetings soon attracted a diverse audience including Cubans and Anglos from various professional backgrounds. The discussion was always free-form and the debates were often heated. The topic could be politics or art or literature or economics. The agenda was as diverse as the audience. Maria would sometimes attend just to enjoy watching and listening to Elena in her true element.

"So, listen," said Elena. "Why don't we use this occasion of your new career as a full-time journalist as an excuse to go out?"

"Oh, Elena. I don't know. I've got so much going on right now."

"Nonsense. When is the last time you saw that guy, Dan, anyway?"

"It's been a while," Maria said guiltily, recalling that she had not returned the last couple calls from Dan.

"I think you should give him a call. I will do the same with Alberto. If it doesn't work out, it will just be us girls for cocktails, say at 7:00 tonight at the Cubana?"

Reluctantly, Maria agreed. Since their initial meeting, Maria and Dan had become friends, with frequent phone calls and occasional meetings for coffee or lunch, as schedules allowed. Lately, however, her schedule had been so intense that she'd been ignoring him. She felt bad for that. Not that Dan hadn't been consumed, too. Working his way through college, he put in long hours on weekends and after classes in a publishing company. After graduating, he planned to sign on full-time with the hopes of becoming a partner in the firm through his sweat equity. Maria tried Dan's number, and was disappointed to find no response.

She had all but given up when her phone rang late that afternoon and she was happy to hear Dan's voice on the line.

"I tried calling you earlier today," she said excitedly. "I'm so glad you called."

"It's great to hear from you again, Maria. It's been way too long," said Dan.

"I have some exciting news," said Maria. "Would you like to get together with Elena and me this evening to celebrate?"

Dan paused before answering. "Funny you should mention celebrating. I was about to tell you some great news, too."

"Really?" she asked. "What's going on?"

"Well, it's actually Alberto's celebration. His parents and sister are out of Cuba. They're here in Miami now, safe and sound."

"How wonderful!" said Maria. "Elena was going to call Alberto, so we can all celebrate together!"

"Actually, I was going to bring somebody," said Dan. "She's a friend who knows Alberto pretty well, too."

Maria's heart sank for an instant, but she quickly

recovered. After all, she thought, they didn't have that type of relationship. But what exactly was their relationship? Obviously they were good friends and she certainly found him attractive, but she had not even returned his last few calls. So why should this news bother her at all?

"That's great," she said. "We can all get together, can't we? By the way, how did Alberto's family manage to get out?"

"I'll explain all that later," said Dan before changing the subject. "Tell me, what's your news?"

"Oh, nothing really. I've been hired as a reporter at the *Herald*. It's official. I start right after graduation."

"Maria, that's wonderful!" Dan said with genuine enthusiasm. "I know that's where you wanted to be and how hard you've worked for it. I can't tell you how happy I am for you. So, it looks like we have a couple of reasons to celebrate this evening."

They settled on the time and place, and Maria hung up the phone thinking how much she enjoyed just hearing Dan's deep resonant voice and mildly chastising herself for letting so much time go by without speaking to or seeing him.

117

Unlike the upscale environment and high energy of South Miami where they had gathered the evening of Maria's birthday, the Cubana was a small restaurant and bar on the edge of Little Havana. Its comfortable surroundings made for a relaxed and casual setting. Dan was already there when Maria arrived, having staked out a booth near the back of the bar area. She felt butterflies again in full force as she walked toward him. Why was that always so, she wondered?

Dan gave Maria a brief hug when she arrived at the booth.

"You're all alone. I thought you were bringing a friend," she said.

"I was," said Dan. "Last minute cancellation. " He smiled and shrugged.

Alberto arrived a few minutes later and was practically beaming when he saw them and quickly sat with them in the booth. His excitement was contagious.

"It has been a great goal for much of my life," he said, "to finally have my family together and out of Cuba."

They had already made it most of the way through an initial round of drinks before Elena arrived apologizing for her lateness.

"So tell me, Alberto" said Maria finally, "how did they get out? Did they have visas?"

118

Alberto looked around conspiratorially. "Well, not exactly," he said.

"I don't understand," said Maria. "Were they able to fly directly into Miami, or did they have to go through Mexico? They obviously didn't come over on a raft."

"No, but you're closer." Alberto paused. "The truth is that I picked them up in my boat two nights ago."

"You did what?" said Maria, astounded. "But... that's not only illegal—it's dangerous!"

"I know. I understand all this. It was something I had to do," said Alberto keeping his voice low and glancing at Dan and Elena.

"My God," said Maria. "I'm glad you're all safe. I mean, it was truly a heroic act on your part to reunite your family, but wasn't it awfully risky?"

Alberto nodded and shrugged.

"How did you manage to do it?" asked Maria, still incredulous. "Aren't there Coast Guard patrols, and what about on the Cuban side? Did you pilot the boat yourself? Did you go over alone?"

"Really, I cannot say anything more," said Alberto faintly smiling.

"Hey, you're starting to act like a real reporter," said Elena, putting down her drink.

"I'm interested," said Maria. "I care about what has happened here."

"Actually," said Alberto, "no one should know of this. I have shared it with you only because you are my friends and I knew you would be happy about its outcome. It should be our secret."

There was a pause in the conversation.

"But why?" asked Maria finally.

"Because," said Alberto calmly, "I might have to do it again."

"What do you mean? Why?" asked Maria.

"I'll tell you why," interjected Elena leaning forward. "Because Castro's tyranny knows no limits; because there are many more as poor or poorer than Alberto's family who have no connections in Cuba or Miami. They have no money, no power, and no future if they stay. Their only other option is to build a raft, and then they would die. Alberto is one of the few, perhaps the only, boat captain who would do this just to help someone. There are many out there who charge thousands of dollars with the promise to smuggle people out.

They are like slave traders. They are scum." She paused. "I'm sorry. It's something I feel passionately about. I can understand why people would do anything to leave a totalitarian system."

"Did you know about this?" Maria asked her.

"No, of course not," said Elena, "but I completely understand it, and I strongly support his actions."

Dan was surprisingly quiet during the conversation.

Maria finally nodded and agreed to keep Alberto's covert activity a secret, all the while knowing it was a compelling story; a son who risks his life to bring his family to freedom. She filed it away with the thought that there might be another angle to this story that she would write about one day. As they all left the restaurant, she and Dan walked out together.

"You knew about all of it, didn't you?" asked Maria in the parking lot.

Dan nodded. "I've known about it since we were eight. That's how long Alberto has been talking about reuniting his family. When it came down to actually doing it, he left me completely out of the picture, though." Dan sighed. "He said he didn't want me involved because it was too risky. But heck, I'm already an accomplice. I knew what he was up to all those months we've been working on that old boat of his,"

Dan said smiling. He looked tired, Maria decided. She suspected that Alberto's quest had definitely worried Dan.

"So, do you really think now that his family is here and safe, Alberto would do this again? Would he take this kind of a risk to rescue strangers?"

"I wouldn't bet against it," said Dan with a tight-lipped nod.

# Chapter Seven

$M$ax Silva, a managing editor at the *Miami Herald*, sat at his desk and reread the memo on his computer screen. He sighed audibly, then picked up his phone and dialed an internal extension.

"Maria? It's Max. How soon can you come over to my office?"

"I see you got my memo," said Maria.

"That's what I want to talk about."

"Okay, give me a couple minutes," said Maria.

Max leaned back and ran his hand through the thinning hair on his middle-aged head. He decided for the umpteenth time that he simply didn't get paid enough for this stuff, not even close. Max could look back on 25 years of his life with the *Herald* that amounted to his entire professional career. In fact, he had hired in not all that long before Maria Montoro. Both had been fresh out of college, young would-be journalists with passionate ideas and hopes. Max had worked his way into management but, somewhere along the way, lost the passion that seemed to drive Maria. She had managed not only to keep the old dreams and hopes, but also to keep coming up with new ones. Maria was now a seasoned reporter with a solid reputation, but she constantly pushed herself, always looking for a new story, a different angle.

"Ready for me?" Maria asked as she leaned her head into Max's office.

"I'm never ready for you, Maria. Come on in," he said motioning her to sit down. "Let's close the door for this one," he added. She raised her eyebrows at this, but closed the door.

"So, how are you, Max? How are things going these days?" asked Maria.

"No, we're not going to do that. We're not going to start acting cordial. Whenever we do that, I get talked into something. Let me just say at the outset that this is one of the craziest notions that anybody has ever walked into my office with. I'd have expected it from some young, wide-eyed journalism student, but not you, Maria. It's a daydream. It's not realistic."

"So," said Maria looking seriously at him, "Are you saying I can't do it?"

"No, I'm saying it can't be done. I'm saying it's not only very difficult to get an interview with Fidel Castro these days, but it's even more so for an American journalist. And even in the unlikely event that he did agree, well, that would only bring up a whole slew of other questions and problems."

Maria sighed. "Max, really, I am sorry that your life is filled with questions and problems. Now tell me again why it was that you decided to get into journalism in the first place, especially since it's chock-full of questions and problems?" Maria smiled, but her eyes were serious.

"Don't start with me, Maria," he said, but she already had. He sighed.

"Okay," he said, "just for kicks, let's review what's on the table. You propose to write an article about the current and future state of Cuba that would include an interview with Fidel Castro. The ground rules that you propose are that the interview would be unrehearsed, with you choosing the questions and not revealing them to him beforehand. You would agree that Castro, or someone he designates, could read the final manuscript before publication to ensure accuracy, but there would be no censoring or other editing allowed.

"What makes you think he would ever agree to such a thing? I don't remember him exactly inviting interviews from what he perceives as a hostile American press corps.

Besides, anything Castro wants to say, he can always put in his own state-run newspaper, *Granma*. Maria, listen to me. I don't think Castro would ever agree to these kinds of ground rules, and if it is perceived as a staged interview, nobody will take it seriously. You've got a reputation out there as one heck of a journalist. Don't throw it away tilting at windmills, or palm trees, or whatever, like some tropical Don Quixote."

"All I'm asking for is permission to try," said Maria. "I think it could be an incredibly important story. People have been writing Castro's obituary for the past 40 some years now. Yet he's still in power, while most of those writers are dead. It's an incredible time of change in Cuba. Tourism now drives the country, for Godsakes. Who'd have seen that coming? Its economy is now three parts totalitarianism, two parts socialism, with a huge black market that Castro silently sanctions.

"In fact, he still calls all the shots. He's an aging dictator, maybe one with an ego bigger than the Caribbean, but he has managed to rule an island just 90 miles from the coast of the most powerful nation on Earth for more than 40 years. He's an enigma. I despise many of his actions, but one cannot help but respect the fact that he is still there. More importantly, at this point in his life, I think he's got to be worried about his legacy and what will happen after his demise. He has an opportunity to offer the people of Cuba a future of prosperity or one of continued poverty.

"And if he should want to talk about his plans for the future, we can offer a much broader podium than he can achieve in anything published in *Granma*. I think he's aware of the power and impact of an objective article as opposed to more propaganda."

"Seriously," Max said, leaning forward and meaning it, "on the obscure chance you could even get this interview, do you realize that you would probably have as many people jeering you as cheering you? I'm worried about your personal safety. I mean it, Maria. There are some in the Miami community with both the means and methods to do harm if they thought you were catering to Castro. In their eyes, you'd be seen as an outright traitor."

"Are we talking about *my* neighborhood, Max? Are you talking about the people I grew up with?" asked Maria. "Let me tell you about the Cuban enclave. It is the antithesis of a monolithic front. If there is one opinion, there is another, and another. We argue all the time, sometimes passionately. One of the things we treasure most about this country is the fact we can say what we think. We can say it out loud; we can argue about it; we can even get it published in the newspaper.

"Look," Maria said finally, "I'm willing to take the consequences for my actions. All I'm asking is for a chance to try this."

Max paused and stared out the window for a moment. "I

don't think you've got a snowball's chance in hell of pulling this off," he said. "But if you can actually get an interview based on those ground rules, go ahead. Go for it."

"Thank you, Max," said Maria.

"Don't thank me," said Max.

Maria was already out the door and walking down the hall when Max called behind her.

"You've already got this whole thing worked out, don't you?" he asked from the doorway of his office. "I'll be damned if you don't."

She turned and smiled broadly, but kept on walking down the hall.

In truth, Maria had put months of effort into the project. She was not surprised by Max's reaction. When she had initially proposed the idea to Elena, she had received much the same discouragement, perhaps in even stronger terms.

While Elena still called Little Havana home, she had become a busy lobbyist, dividing her time between Washington, D.C. and Miami. It had taken Maria some doing to convince her, but once convinced, she agreed to use her connections to make some of the initial inquiries. Despite the fact that Elena lobbied for the Cuban exile community in

Miami, she still maintained contacts within Cuba, some even within the government. As she put it, "One must know one's adversaries in order to defeat them."

It had been tedious going at first. Despite Maria's solid journalistic reputation and Elena's connections, authorities in Havana had summarily denied the initial request. Slowly, however, Elena worked her "back-channel" resources, and a dialogue finally commenced.

However, even when the Cuban government authorities tentatively agreed to an interview with Castro, they insisted that all questions be submitted and approved in advance. This requirement was grudgingly lifted when Elena argued that Maria had conducted interviews with various Latin American heads of state based on those same ground rules, and to a person, all agreed she had been fair in the stories she had written.

On more than one occasion, the talks seemed to grind to a halt and Maria doubted the project would ever come to fruition, but eventually the unlikely interview was arranged with all of Maria's ground rules intact. Finally, a date was agreed upon. As Max had suspected, the meeting with him had been a formality.

The chartered twin-engine craft lifted off from Miami for the approximately 100-mile flight to Havana on an April morning in 2003 under clear blue skies. It banked west in a broad circle before heading south across the Straits of Florida with its pilots and three passengers: Maria, a photographer from the *Herald*, and Elena.

Maria looked out the window as they flew over the expanse of sparkling blue waters, then turned to Elena and said, "So, it's really going to happen, isn't it?"

"It's about time," said Elena. "You've been ready for weeks."

Maria nodded and returned to the view out the window, her thoughts going back to the last time she crossed these waters. It seemed like so long ago now, yet memories of Cuba filled her mind. Events she hadn't thought about in years came back to her with remarkable clarity, but it was as if they had happened to someone else, not her. It really had been another life.

Focusing, Maria turned her thoughts to the interview and began rereading one of her many briefing books. During the months of negotiations, she had spent endless hours researching in preparation for the interview. She had delved into Castro's personal history, studying everything from his childhood to his university years to his rise to power. She came prepared to talk about events as old as the Bay of Pigs and the Cuban missile crisis to Elián Gonzáles to as recent as Castro's crackdown on dissidents or the execution of three men by firing squad for attempting to hijack a ferry. She was ready to discuss the ongoing trade embargo, education, religion, civil rights, and Castro's staunch unwillingness to allow any real democratic reform in Cuba, while at the same time allowing various forms of capitalism to take root when it suited him.

Elena, who had played the role of mentor, coach, and debate partner to Maria over the past few months, had insisted on accompanying her for the planned three-day session, despite Maria's protests. As always, Elena had made no attempt to hide her strong opinions while freely giving Maria advice.

"Make sure you don't let him intimidate you. And do not let him pretend to befriend you. And above all, do not let him get away with long rambling answers that hide the truth. It is a favorite tactic. He will pile answers upon answers until the question itself is obscured."

"Yes, yes, okay," said Maria, feeling exasperated. "You act like this is my first interview."

"It *is* your first interview with *him*," Elena answered.

A little over thirty minutes after take-off, the plane banked as it approached the coast of Cuba. Looking out the window, Maria could see Havana's harbor and the old city below. As they made their final approach, she almost expected the see Uncle Vicente in his white linen suit, waving a handkerchief to greet her return, although he had passed away many years ago.

When they taxied to a halt on the tarmac, two guards and a protocol officer were waiting for them. There was also an official government interpreter who was introduced as Eva, although one was hardly necessary as Maria and Elena both spoke fluent Spanish. After their paperwork was processed, the protocol officer informed them that they would first be taken to their hotel where they would have lunch. They would be contacted when the President was ready.

On their drive through the city, Maria was at once reminded of the beauty of old Havana, now sadly faded. The paint-barren buildings that lined the streets still tried to hold on to the vestiges of their stately past. Many were so decrepit and crumbling, however, that Maria suspected they were already beyond repair. She recalled traversing some of these same streets with her father the day before they had left Havana. Now, almost forty years later, she found that while little had changed physically, the charm of the capital was tarnished by decay and poverty.

Their hotel, housed in an old and once-elegant building,

was on a corner in one of the oldest sections of Havana. Inside, large glass chandeliers lit the lobby, and the carpet, though worn, was of high quality. A porter carried their bags to the elevator, which they took to the fourth floor. The suite was large and open with tall windows looking out at other old buildings. Off the central living area were separate entrances to the three single bedrooms.

Maria had hoped they could begin the interview soon after lunch, but this was not to be the case. Their interpreter Eva informed them that their official schedule would first include a guided tour of the old sections of Havana. They finally returned to the hotel suite in the middle of the afternoon, where they anxiously waited for a call that did not come.

Maria and Elena made small talk while the *Herald* photographer Alec played solitaire. Maria watched Eva as she quietly jotted down notes in a small pad from time to time and began to suspect that acting as an interpreter for two Spanish-speaking former citizens was not necessarily Eva's only assignment while in their company.

By late afternoon, Elena's impatience became evident. "I've had it with this stalling tactic," she said as she went over to the phone. "I'm going to find out what's going on."

Eventually, Eva excused herself and ventured down to the lobby, presumably to make inquiries of her own. A half-hour later, Elena hung up the phone with an exasperated sigh.

"I can't get anybody to give me a straight answer," she said.

Eva finally returned with the news that the president was having an extremely busy day, and that there would be no opportunity for an interview.

"But we're only here for three days," said Maria, now also growing exasperated and not a little worried.

"I am aware of your schedule," said Eva calmly. She paused and then explained that despite Castro's busy schedule, he had invited Maria—and Maria only—to join him for dinner that evening. There could be no photographers and no lobbyists she said by way of a less than sincere apology to Elena and Alec.

"*El Comandante* would like an opportunity to get a little bit acquainted with Ms. Montoro prior to the actual interview," Eva said.

Elena was livid at the news, and suggested in strong terms that they get on the plane and return to Miami immediately.

"This kind of manipulation is unacceptable!" she said vehemently. "It changes the agreement and I think ends the possibility of an interview."

"Listen," Maria said. "Exactly who will be present and when will this take place?" Unlike Elena, she was not anxious to see her story disappear so quickly.

"My understanding is that it will only be you and the president. A car and driver will be sent for you at seven o'clock and will take you to the Presidential Palace," said Eva.

"And the conversation will be considered off-the-record?"

"Yes, I'm afraid so," said Eva.

"Okay, I'll do it," said Maria with finality.

Eva soon departed, saying she would be back in an hour to escort Elena and Alec to a separate dinner with her. After she left, Elena sat heavily in one of the upholstered chairs in the common area of the suite and kicked off her shoes, lighting a cigarette. "I don't like it, Maria; an unaccompanied and off-the-record meeting with Castro. I don't like it at all."

"Look at it this way," Maria responded, "It may be just what is needed to set the tone for the interview. I think this may give us an opportunity to avoid starting out in a confrontational manner. It may allow us to build on a certain common ground, a certain understanding, which could promote a more meaningful exchange. After all, if the interview is only a recitation of policy statements, well, it won't really be worth much, will it?"

Elena paused and finally nodded. "I suppose not. But I

can't help feeling that he's setting you up. He's changing the game rules right at the outset."

"Don't worry," said Maria. "What do you think he's going to do?"

"That's the point," said Elena. "I can't even guess what he might be up to."

At 7:30 that evening, there was a knock on the door of the suite. Elena and Alec had left some twenty minutes before with Eva and Maria was alone in the suite. She opened the door to find a Cuban guard in a dress uniform standing in the hallway. He was young, perhaps twenty, and very serious. He bowed decorously and told Maria that the limousine was waiting for her.

Maria put her shawl over the shoulders of her black business suit, picked up her Chanel purse, and followed him to the elevator. She had considered an evening dress, but dismissed it. Despite the supposed informal nature of this meeting, she wanted to send a signal that it was going to be all business.

Outside, a chauffeur waited beside an ancient Mercedes limousine. She thought it could well have been the very one she had seen Castro in so many years ago. After closing

Maria's door, the guard sat up front as the chauffeur expertly navigated the limousine through a maze of narrow streets, finally pulling to a stop in front of the Presidential Palace.

Another guard met them at the door. He checked her purse, removing her hand-held tape recorder, but made no attempt to search her further. He led her down a broad hallway and up a wide, sweeping set of stairs. There, yet another guard opened a door off the hallway and motioned for her to enter.

Standing just beyond in the doorway was Fidel Castro.

He was tall, even more so than she had remembered. The years had considerably whitened his hair and beard, and his face seemed more drawn, the cheekbones harder. His eyes were piercing, though they now had slight bags under them. He was not wearing his trademark military garb, nor a suit and tie. Instead, he had on a more informal guayabera shirt, open at the neck, with short sleeves.

Maria was taken a little aback when he bowed and briefly kissed her hand. There's no denying his charm and charisma, she thought. He greeted her in English, but soon lapsed into Spanish, casually inquiring about her trip to Havana and if her accommodations were comfortable. He made no apology for the delay or the change in plans that resulted in the two of them standing alone in his office. He mentioned only that his schedule of late was quite demanding.

His office was large and ornate. Maria noticed a collage of photos that occupied one wall with other framed photos placed on tables and shelves here and there, many the familiar faces of various world leaders. A doorway off to the side led to a small private dining area where a table had been set for them. While they continued their polite chatter, Castro led her into the room where he sat down after seating her.

Maria finally had to ask him, "Could you tell me why just the two of us are here having dinner, as opposed to a more formal interview situation?"

"I want to know you as a person," he said, "before engaging in an interview."

He then launched into a discourse concerning the importance of objective journalism, with his specific criticisms of a number of major journalists, especially television journalists, whom he called "media personalities." He had gone on for some fifteen minutes when he paused and suddenly looked quite pale. Seemingly from out of nowhere, an attendant, who Maria thought to be a doctor or a male nurse, quickly appeared and brought him a pill with a glass of water. Castro said nothing for a few moments, but then picked up where he had left off with no explanation of the interruption.

He turned his attention to Maria's work, and it was quickly evident to her that he had read almost everything she had ever published. He was complimentary, but not overly so.

"I understand your family comes from the area of Las Tunas," he said finally.

"Yes," Maria said. "We left in 1965 after my father's plantation was taken from us," to which Castro did not respond.

"Do you still have family in Cuba?" he asked.

Maria nodded, but felt immediately uncomfortable talking about any family members remaining in Cuba.

"And your family, the ones who left, they have no regrets?"

"It was difficult in the beginning, but no, there are no regrets. The opportunity to live in freedom was worth it."

Castro did not respond.

"You know," Maria said, "I have seen you once before in person, on an evening just before my family and I left Havana. There was a motorcade, and a jeep hit a car at an intersection not far from this palace. You got out of your limousine and shouted for your guards to move the car out of the way. They pulled the driver from the car and beat him before tipping the car over on its side so you could pass."

Castro shrugged. "These are but the memories of a child. I have no such recollection."

"Do you perhaps remember a man named Fernando García from Santiago de Cuba? He was tried and imprisoned after the Bay of Pigs invasion. His son, José García, was a member of Brigade 2506, and died in one of your prisons. Fernando was a close friend of my father's who asked me to determine his fate while I was here, if that should be possible."

Castro listened attentively, while watching Maria closely. His eyes never moved. There was no hint of emotion. He finally said, "No, I do not recall a Fernando García or his son. These events happened long ago, and the records are sometimes incomplete. I will check on this," he added, but made no attempt to write anything down.

"Thank you," said Maria.

A middle-aged waiter appeared in the private dining room, bringing Maria a small, but well-prepared meal consisting of baked chicken, rice and vegetables with a glass of white wine. Interestingly, she noted Castro was served only brown rice and vegetables and he drank only bottled water.

Over dinner, and for a good hour afterwards, Castro questioned Maria about the various interviews she had conducted with other Latin American leaders over the years, asking many details as to how the interviews were handled and her impressions of the subjects. He also inquired into many aspects of life in the United States, seeking out her views on healthcare, poverty, race relations, and education, among others.

Despite his reputation for talkativeness and a tendency to dominate any conversation, Castro seemed genuinely curious about her thoughts and impressions and peppered her with follow-up questions. By the end of the evening, Maria felt she had surely been the one interviewed that night.

She mentioned this in parting, but Castro waved off the comment, saying only, "Tomorrow will be your turn for questions. Tonight, we have gotten to know each other a little, yes? Good night."

Elena was waiting up for her when Maria returned to the suite at the hotel. She sat on the couch smoking a cigarette as Maria closed the door.

"So?" Elena asked impatiently.

"It was quite strange," Maria said, sitting down, waving the smoke away from her face. "You really need to kick that habit," she added, mildly chastising Elena who ignored her. "To be honest, he wasn't anything like I would have imagined; not from the other interviews I read and not from what I've seen of him on video. It was quite unexpected, really."

Maria went on to relay the events of the evening to Elena, who listened attentively, occasionally asking for more details. When Maria was finished, Elena crushed out another cigarette and stood.

"You see what he's doing, don't you? He's playing the part of the benevolent great uncle, lulling you into a passive mode, while he gathers whatever information he can to use against you."

"Against me?" asked Maria. "I told him nothing that he could possibly use against me."

"He wanted to see your interview techniques first-hand; he asked about how you approached other leaders you have interviewed; he wanted to know what you thought about their personalities and responses. It sure sounds like a scouting mission to me. Don't you see? He's already got you made. Do you think he honestly wanted to know your perspective about life in America? Or did you forget for a moment that you were talking to a dyed-in-the-wool communist?"

Maria pondered this for a moment before saying, "Yes, he might have been laying the groundwork to anticipate my questions. You could be right about that, but there was something else. Strangely, I think he was actually interested in hearing my perspective on life in the U.S., and how we are approaching some of these problems."

"Honestly, Maria. You don't think he gets CNN or Fox News? The man does nothing that is not calculated to serve his own self interest," said Elena. "Believe me on this."

It was a different Castro who appeared before all of them when they arrived at the Presidential Palace the next morning. Wearing his standard green military uniform and polished black books, he greeted them formally, almost gruffly.

Instead of his office, the interview was conducted in one of the formal palace rooms. Two aides and the interpreter Eva were also present. Alec, the *Herald* photographer, quietly moved about the room, his camera making mechanical clicking and whirring sounds as he snapped photos.

Maria and Castro sat in chairs with a side table between them. There were flowers on the table along with two glasses of water. She poised herself before beginning, then switched on her tape recorder and placed it on the table.

"Thank you for the opportunity to speak with you today, *Comandante*. It's been well over forty years now since you came to power in Cuba. Since that time, and especially lately, there have been many changes in Cuba. How do you characterize the state of the revolution that you inspired?"

"You give me too much credit," said Castro. "I am simply the leader of a team. As to the state of the revolution, it is in excellent shape. As just one example," he said leaning forward, "our leadership in medical schooling has made us a world leader. Cuba now has more doctors per capita than any other nation on Earth. And this is based on internationally recognized statistics."

"True, there are many doctors in Cuba, but aren't there many hospitals also lacking even the most basic drugs to dispense? While the general populace has to go without, high-ranking officials or tourists able to pay with American dollars have access to treatment."

"This is a falsehood," said Castro defiantly. " In Cuba everyone has access to medical care and medicines and they do not pay a penny for this."

"Perhaps more to the point," said Maria, "why does Cuba even need so many doctors? Is it not a waste of the available financial resources to fund so many doctors while being unable to furnish such necessities as electricity, food and even clean drinking water?"

But Castro would have none of it. He maintained that his immense corps of doctors was a viable symbol of the revolution's success, just as Cuba's education system and the country's literacy rate of 96 percent were indicators that his brand of socialism was working.

"But why are so many educated people having to go hungry?" asked Maria. "With so many educated people, why is it not possible for a more prosperous society to have been created in Cuba?"

"This is a complicated issue," said Castro, stroking his beard. "The U.S. embargo has been in effect for over forty years now, a persecution that the Cuban people have endured with remarkable courage. Added to this was the collapse of the Soviet Union and the socialist block. Despite these intense economic hardships, we have maintained our economy, and have sought other economic markets. In addition to educating thousands of new doctors who are now part of our healthcare system, we have kept open our schools and clinics. Given these realities, I think the Cuban economy has survived very well. One must remember that we are a poor country compared to the United States, but unlike the United States, we have distributed our resources much more equitably."

Maria asked, "I am certain that the sanctions no doubt caused large losses to the Cuban economy, but why has there not been more progress made in the course of the thirty-some years of Soviet subsidies that amounted to more than $100 billion? Wasn't it simply that the system didn't work, regardless of the sanctions?"

"One must understand that the economy of Cuba is quite different from that in the U.S. They cannot be compared.

The vast majority of Cubans do not pay for the homes they live in, nor do they pay taxes for them. And those that do pay are only charged a very low rent. Our medicines, food and other essential goods are not taxed and basic foodstuffs are subsidized so that all may have access to them."

Maria and Castro sparred through the morning, the conversation sometimes becoming intense. By mid-afternoon Castro looked visibly fatigued, and Maria wondered if there would be another occurrence like the one the evening before. But he insisted on continuing. For every question he had a ready answer, for every argument he had a counter-argument.

Maria was unhappy to see where the interview was going. There would be no "winning" points in a discussion with this Fidel Castro. He clearly felt he was on stage and insisted on having the last word on any subject brought up. His logic would be the only logic accepted.

"I'd like to ask about the *balseros*," said Maria, "the many people who have taken desperate measures and risked their lives to leave Cuba. Why is it that over a million Cubans have fled the island since the revolution? Why is it that today one out of every six Cubans lives abroad? And how many more would leave if they could get a visa or afford the trip?"

"Our doors have always been open. No one has been prevented from emigrating from Cuba to the United States," said Castro. "It is the United States that has closed its doors on various occasions, which has encouraged illegal emigration. Giving any Cuban who reaches U.S. soil the right to residency only encourages criminal activity. It is a policy of aggression and hostility that is directed only at Cuba. The worst are the perpetrators who illegally provide a means for misguided Cubans to try to cross the Straits of Florida. These worms should be prosecuted to the full extent of the law."

"And the three men who were just recently executed for having tried to hijack a Havana ferry with the hopes of reaching the United States?" asked Maria.

"These men were terrorists and were tried and convicted of those charges. They were part of a larger plot to attempt to destabilize the legitimate government of Cuba," said Castro.

Finally, Maria got to the question of Castro's longevity. "Considering your age, you must admit that you will not be able to serve forever," she said. "What do you see as the future of Cuba after your departure?"

"I never think about death," said Castro. "I am not one of your media personalities, but only an ordinary Cuban citizen. Therefore, there is no need for a successor, nor will there be a need for a transition after my death. The revolution that has been successful for more than forty years will continue in the same manner that it has. The future of Cuba is self evident."

Maria could see there was no changing course for Castro. There would be no dramatic reforms. His positions were cast as hard as a stone statue in a park, and were just as unflinching. While he may ask questions and listen in private, in public it would always be a one-way conversation. His version of the future of Cuba was a continuation of Castro, and whatever it took to make that happen would happen.

The interview ended in the early evening with Maria feeling exhausted. They had been ushered to the central lobby of the palace and were preparing to depart when a guard hurriedly approached Maria.

"The *Comandante* would like to see you briefly," he said in her ear.

Surprised, Maria left Elena and Alec with Eva and followed the guard up the stairs. Castro was alone in his office standing near the bookshelf as she entered.

"So," he said, "I did not do too badly for an old man, yes?"

Maria shrugged and said, "I enjoyed our conversation more last night. Today was, well, more of a debate."

"Obviously your views are quite different than mine, and that was evident today," he said. "I trust you will offer me the same fair treatment that you have done for others in past interviews."

"Of course," Maria said, "I always do that."

"Very well," he said, going to his desk and opening a manila folder. "I have some information for you about one Fernando García. He was a counter-revolutionary spy who was tried following the Bay of Pigs invasion. For his treasonous acts, he was sentenced to 30 years in prison. I personally reduced the sentence to 5 years based on his age and health. Unfortunately, he died of natural causes within the first year of his sentence. I am sorry."

He closed the folder. "I have done this as a courtesy," he said.

"Thank you for the information," said Maria and then paused. "Would it be possible for me to visit his grave?"

"The cemetery is within the prison, and I am afraid visitors are not allowed," Castro said.

"I see," Maria said finally. "Then I guess I should be going."

Castro nodded. "Perhaps we will have an opportunity to talk again one day. I will look forward to reading your article." He came to her and formally kissed her hand as he had on the occasion of their first meeting.

Maria looked in his eyes as he raised his head back up, and she saw a certain fierceness in them that scared her. Castro may be many things, but he was nobody's benevolent uncle; of that she was certain. But behind that fierceness, she saw only darkness. He would remain a mystery to her.

"What was that all about?" asked Elena when Maria caught up with them outside the palace.

"I had asked for information about an old friend of our family," Maria said, "only the news was not good."

The incident came up again a couple weeks later, when Maria hosted a small party at her house to celebrate the publication of her piece on Castro. Elena, Dan and Alberto were among the guests. A Gypsy Kings CD was playing in the background as they casually talked in the family room. She and Elena were telling them some of the details about the Castro interview and their experience in Havana.

"And then, just as we were leaving, Castro sent a guard downstairs to bring Maria back up to his office. Honestly, we were all but getting into the limousine," said Elena.

"What did he want?" asked Dan.

"Oh, it was a personal request," said Maria, pausing before going on. "I asked him about the fate of a man who was an old friend of my father's and helped our family leave Cuba.

He was strongly anti-Castro and supported the Bay of Pigs invasion. His son was part of Brigade 2506 and died soon after the conflict due to injuries he sustained on the beach. We knew my father's friend had been arrested and imprisoned, but we never learned his final fate. Castro called me back to his office to tell me our friend had died in prison within the first year. I have a picture of him," Maria said walking over to the bookshelf and picking up a framed photo. "His name was Fernando García."

There was a moment's silence before Alberto said, "My God," taking the framed picture from her. He held it in his hands and stared at it unbelievingly.

"This photo, it's the person who met me at the airport when I arrived here." He turned to Dan and said, "This was the archangel who saved me as a young boy."

"But that's impossible," said Maria. "He died in Cuba. He never made it over here."

"When did he die?" asked Alberto.

"It must have been sometime in 1961, I would think," said Maria.

"The same year I arrived here," said Alberto, now nodding his head, still staring at the photo. "This was the man who helped me. I'm sure of it. His soul must have stopped in Miami on its way to heaven. I understand that now."

Maria smiled with her eyebrows raised and looked to Dan, who shrugged as if to say he didn't know what to make of it either. Meanwhile, Alberto carefully placed the photo back on the shelf, treating it like a holy relic.

# Chapter
# Eight

T hey were supposed to meet at a little restaurant off S.W. Eighth Street, better known as *Calle Ocho*, in Miami's Little Havana. It was just past eleven o'clock on a Thursday morning when Dan showed up, a little early for lunch, a little late for brunch; so he decided to look for a parking space near the restaurant and wait.

Not that he minded the wait. Dan looked forward to his weekly lunches with Alberto. They always met in Little Havana. He loved the music, the sights, and the smells. Most of all, perhaps, he loved the energy that exuded from the place and the activity that seemingly went on there all the time. It combined to give him a sense of being immersed in an exotic Latin culture, far from anything one could imagine existing on the U.S. mainland.

He pulled his Saab over to the curb and checked for messages from the office on his cell phone, then walked up the street and sat at a small table. Alberto would no doubt be running late. Dan glanced at his watch as the waitress brought a cup of Cuban espresso over and casually sat down across from him.

"So, where is your Spanish brother today, Danny? You are always early and he is always late. It's a wonder you ever meet," she chided him good-naturedly.

Dan smiled and nodded his head. It was true. Alberto was never one to be held hostage to a schedule. Conversely, Dan's life was run by schedules, or rather, he ran the schedules. As a successful publisher and printer, he created schedules, he met schedules, and he rearranged them when he had to. It was a business he loved, but one that demanded precise timing. There were always deadlines and as the old adage went, a printer is only as good as his last job.

Although they had been classmates up through high school, Alberto chose not to go to college. He currently made a modest living taking people out on charter cruises. He lived on his boat at the marina. For Alberto, "home" was an extremely fast, beautiful, and well-outfitted 35-foot cigarette boat he christened as *Miguel*. "Like the archangel," he would say, "always ready to protect the innocent."

"He'll be along in his own good time, I'm sure, Lili. What's with this weather, anyway?" Dan asked squinting up at the sky. What had started as a beautiful day was quickly clouding over.

"It's going to be some bad weather coming our way, I hear," she said brushing off her skirt as she stood. "You're going to be fine eating outside for lunch, if your friend ever comes. But tonight, well, that may be another story."

Dan leisurely sipped his espresso and waited another 15 minutes before trying to call Alberto. There was no answer but this did not surprise him. Despite having state-of-the-art navigation and every communication gadget possible on board *Miguel*, Alberto was notorious for ignoring phone calls if he was otherwise occupied.

Dan was just about to go ahead and order when his cell phone chimed.

"It looks like you're going to have to have a Cuban sandwich and your black bean soup without me today," said Alberto. "My less-than-graceful first mate had a little run in with a grappling hook, and the hook won. I'm on my way to the hospital now. He will live to fish another day, but I'm afraid it won't be today. So, his clumsiness has cost me lunch with you. How are you doing, anyway, little brother?"

Dan smiled at the "little brother" reference coming from the smaller of the two. He said he was fine and not to worry about lunch. Although Alberto had made light of the incident, Dan thought he detected a tenseness in his voice.

"What about dinner tonight?" he asked. "If you're going to skip out on lunch with me, at least I can make sure you have one decent meal today."

There was a pause before Alberto replied. "Don't think so, little brother. Something came up. I have a little charter tour scheduled this evening and, um, I think I may have my hands full... Maybe next week, though, for lunch, for sure. Okay, amigo?"

Dan felt the hair on the back of his head stand up. He knew exactly what Alberto was talking about. It had nothing to do with a last-minute charter and everything to do with breaking the law, and Alberto risking his life.

For some time now, Dan knew Alberto had been engaged in the dangerous and illegal activity of moving small groups of Cuban refugees across the treacherous Straits of Florida. It started with the vow to bring his family over, a quest that had taken him more than 15 years, but he had accomplished it.

Alberto, who always felt at home on the sea, had managed to buy a used boat in his early twenties. It was a worn and rundown and barely seaworthy wreck, but with Dan's help, they repaired it and, over a period of months, amazingly brought it back to life. When they finished it, Alberto christened it *Miguel*, as he would christen every boat he owned in life. By Dan's count, the current one was the seventh *Miguel*.

Despite his youth and inexperience at the time, Alberto had always had an innate ability to navigate the sea. The type of vessel didn't matter much. He could sail a ship or pilot a motorboat or navigate a raft. It was no surprise that soon after the restoration was complete, he had quietly begun to work on his secret project, his plan to rescue his family. He studied navigation charts and the routines of Coast Guard vessels. He talked to people in the exile community who knew about such things. He listened and he learned.

Alberto would be the first to point out that the initial voyage a year later was mostly a matter of beginner's luck. He managed to evade the U.S. Coast Guard, traverse the Straits of Florida, slip through Cuban coastal defenses, pick up his father, mother and sister, and make the return trip safely and without incident.

Over the course of the next twenty-five years, Alberto would make other trips. Unlike the corrupt smugglers who profited off the miseries of a trapped people, he never took a single peso or dollar for his efforts. Because of this, he became known to those who mattered in the Cuban-American community as a man of integrity, and a much-sought-after resource.

Alberto was prudent. He picked his times and places and passengers carefully. He turned down many more pleas than he accepted. Because money was never the object, he could not be bought. Usually, he helped those people in the most dire need. He would listen to the request, hear the story, and check the facts. And if everything checked out, only then would he agree to help.

Alberto always made the three-hour run from South Florida to Cuba late at night, using to his advantage both the cover of darkness and the fact that his boat sat so low in the water that it was difficult to pick up on radar. There were still many dangers, though, even with the latest in communications equipment, global positioning technology, and night vision goggles. One still had to evade the U.S. Coast Guard both departing and returning to Florida's shores. There were also Drug Enforcement Agency planes monitoring maritime traffic. The Cuban coastal protection forces, the Border Guard, might not be as technologically advanced as their U.S. counterparts, but they were much more deadly. They would not think twice about firing on and sinking a rogue vessel, thereby saving the time and inconvenience of a trial.

Between the Cuban and U.S. shores, there was also the possibility of encountering drug runners or any of a variety of modern-day pirates or smugglers who, given the opportunity, would be happy to steal a boat like Alberto's after killing everyone onboard. And then there were the sharks, notorious in the Straits of Florida.

If everything worked out as it was supposed to, Alberto would make the nighttime crossing in his well-rigged boat without incident. He would navigate to a prearranged rendezvous point, usually an obscure beach, where he would slow the boat to a crawl. Then he would wait for a code signal via flashlight to be made from the shore, an agreed-upon number of flashes, some short, some long. He would return the signal in kind. Only after this scenario played out flawlessly would Alberto approach the beach to within wading distance of the shoreline. The slightest deviation would be cause for him to abruptly go to full throttle and disappear into the darkness. As risky as this business was, Alberto took as few chances as possible.

"The daring boat captains are all dead, my friend. It's only the cautious ones like me who live to make up the stories," he would say, and laugh, exposing his white teeth and broad grin.

Dan, however, was not smiling now. "A tour tonight, you said, alone? You've still got to eat. How about if I bring you some take-out."

"Better make it early then. I've got some work to do," said Alberto.

Dan made it through the afternoon, although he was distracted. Over the years, he had helped Alberto by quietly financing his covert trips, but Dan had always felt uneasy about it. Not because he didn't believe it was the right thing to do, but because he worried about Alberto's safety. Yet Dan knew that despite Alberto's seemingly casual attitude, he was a serious and thorough planner, and a cautious and expert ship captain.

What bothered Dan most was the thought of Alberto making this trip alone tonight. His first mate, Juan, had been a trusted friend for many years. Obviously, Alberto could not simply replace him. Dan hoped to convince Alberto to postpone the endeavor. If that were not possible, Dan was determined to accompany him. While not being in the same league with Alberto when it came to piloting a boat, Dan was by no means inexperienced. He and Alberto often went boating together, usually with their respective dates, but sometimes just the two of them. It gave them a chance to talk away from the bustle of their respective schedules. Dan knew enough about boating and about Alberto's secret operations to know that his boyhood friend should not try to do it alone.

After his last appointment, Dan swung by his apartment and quickly threw some clothes in a bag. In the last moment, he grabbed his foul-weather gear out of the closet and took it with him. As he walked back out to the car, he looked up at the ominously clouding sky. He didn't like the looks of the weather, not one bit.

On his way back across town, he stopped and got some Chinese take-out, curry chicken for him, and the vegetarian dish called Buddha's Feast, for Alberto. It was a little after six when he pulled into the marina. He saw Alberto loading life preservers into the forward hatch of the bow over the V-hull of the long and narrow cigarette boat. As ever, he was struck by the boat's elegance and the ease at which Alberto moved about it.

Alberto looked up and watched Dan approach. "Hey, amigo, do you think you're moving in?" he said, eyeing Dan's gym bag and folded foul-weather gear.

"Actually, I was hoping to talk you into keeping *Miguel* anchored right here tonight. Maybe you and I could play a couple rounds of cards and watch a little late night TV."

"Not a chance, amigo," said Alberto seriously. "I have a rendezvous that must be kept," he said lowering his voice, as he took the bag containing the Chinese food and Dan maneuvered himself off the dock and onto the boat while balancing his gear.

Down below, Alberto told Dan the details. He had been contacted by one of his trusted sources in the Cuban exile community.

"The pick-up is a doctor and his family. He will almost surely be arrested in the morning. We need to get him out tonight.

"What happened?" asked Dan.

"He criticized the Cuban government for the lack of medicine he needed to treat a patient. Of course he was just pointing out the obvious," said Alberto. "There hasn't been real medicine in Havana for years. Castro graduates a thousand doctors, but gives them little more than aspirin to dispense. So what do you have? Thousands of frustrated doctors, that's what. This doctor complained about it. He just happened to complain to the wrong person. It sucks. But I need to pull them out tonight. There can be no rearrangement of the schedule."

"Have you looked at the weather?" asked Dan, sitting down on one of the padded benches under the narrow glass slit of a window.

"I know," said Alberto. "It's not as good as I would like. And it could get worse tonight. I've been monitoring the weather band."

"How's Juan?" Dan asked changing the subject.

"He'll be fine in a couple days. The grappling hook missed the artery, but he still bled like a pig."

"Listen, you can't do this alone, Alberto. You know that, right?"

"I know I'm going to do what I have to do," said Alberto, his tone matching Dan's sudden seriousness. "And you're not about to go with me, amigo. If that's even remotely what you are thinking, that will not be possible."

Dan rarely saw Alberto's temper, but when it surfaced, he could lash out with surprising intensity. Dan felt he might be close to that point.

"Look," said Dan. "We both know this is important to you. But even on a good day with a first mate, it's a risky endeavor. To go out alone and in poor weather sounds crazy to me—and it must to you, too. Come on Alberto, I know you would not put these people in any more risk than you had to."

"They're already at risk. If I don't get them out tonight, there may not be a tomorrow, at least for the doctor," said Alberto.

"Then I'm going with you. It's that simple. I may not be as good as Juan, but I know how to pilot this boat, I can navigate as well as anybody you know and, most of all, you trust me as much as I trust you. And I trust you with my life."

Dan didn't know if Alberto's look was one of resignation or relief, but he sat down heavily in the captain's chair by the navigation charts. "My sources tell me this man, this doctor, this healer, is as good as dead when they arrest him in the morning. I don't like going out in this weather. I am no fool. But this time around I have no choice, amigo. I'm their last hope."

Alberto eyed Dan steadily. "And now our Chinese food is getting cold. Juan costs me lunch and now you cost me a hot dinner. There is no respect for this boat captain," said Alberto finally grinning. Dan grinned back.

"So it's settled then," said Dan. "You've got yourself a first mate for this tour."

Dan had no sooner opened the bag that his friend had set down earlier than Alberto dove into the boxed Chinese dinners and began eating voraciously. They finished the meals in a matter of minutes while going over some of the details of the trip. They talked like men who knew each other well and had done this before. Various aspects of the journey would be the same as any other time they had taken *Miguel* out into the ocean, but there were serious and dangerous differences. This time it would be an illegal run across the Florida Straits. It would be nighttime. And there was the weather.

Within a couple hours, they had stowed everything and gone over the navigation chart in detail. "We must be very careful here and here," said Alberto pointing out two specific points off the coast of Florida. "It's regularly patrolled by the Coast Guard." Dan nodded and made a mental note.

Meanwhile, the weather band radio continued to crackle in the background as it repeatedly announced small craft warnings for South Florida. Although not yet raining, the clouds were building and the stars were no longer visible. The wind had also picked up some from the southwest. They'd be traveling into a headwind on their way there, but it should hopefully be to their back on the way home.

The last thing they did before leaving was motor over to the fuel dock and fill up both the main and auxiliary tanks on *Miguel*. Alberto checked the gauges twice and satisfied, signaled Dan to untie the boat as he started the powerful engines and they made their way out of the marina and into Biscayne Bay.

The bay was choppy, but they made good progress across it. Alberto was careful to follow the buoys, traveling not too fast, nor too slow. For this part of the journey, he left his running lights on. Later on, they would go into a stealth mode. Leaving the bay, Alberto increased the throttle and the boat fairly rocketed over the waves. Dan could not help but be impressed by the power of Alberto's craft every time they went out.

Having run parallel to the shoreline for some time, they continued due south and headed out into the open sea and the Straits of Florida where the weather worsened. The waves were cresting higher and the wind had increased in strength. Dan monitored the weatherband radio and made continuous checks of the GPS to verify their exact position. Alberto stayed at the helm, cold water splashing him every now and again, while he maintained a steady speed and course. He didn't mind. He could have simply turned on the autopilot and left it to the computerized navigation system, but Alberto preferred to have his hands on the wheel.

Three hours later, they were within 12 miles of the Cuban coast. Alberto cut the running lights and slowed down. From here on in, it would be a covert mission. Dan switched the radio to the specific frequency that Alberto told him to, one that would pick up any conversations from the Cuban coastal defense forces or patrol boats. It began to rain harder and the waves were getting higher.

They were heading to a precise point on a beach near Santa Cruz del Norte, about 10 miles from Guanabacoa. If all went as planned, a family of six would be waiting for them, cowering in the tall grass, wet, scared, and anxious.

Dan took a deep breath and went back up on the deck. It was time to get down to business.

Late in the afternoon at a warehouse in a run-down marina in south Florida, Maria looked at her watch and waited for her contact to appear, a shadowy figure she only knew as Vincent, which was no doubt not his real name.

The story she was writing was about the trade of smuggling people out of Cuba. It was one that had been "percolating," as she put it, for some time now, perhaps ever since she had learned of Alberto's venture to rescue his family from Cuba.

In the two decades since then, conditions in Cuba had only gotten worse, and a burgeoning industry had developed made up of smugglers taking advantage of emigrants desperate to leave Cuba and willing to pay large amounts of cash for the possibility of a boat ride to freedom. From $500 to $10,000 per head was not unheard of, depending upon the seaworthiness of the craft.

A change in U.S. policy in 1994 made it even more attractive to would-be smugglers. Prior to then, any Cuban refugees who made it to U.S. territorial waters, meaning out to 12 miles from shore, were considered political exiles and usually eligible to enter the U.S. That year the U.S. instituted the "wet-foot/dry-foot" policy that decreed only those Cuban refugees who physically touched U.S. soil could remain in the country. A refugee apprehended at sea was returned to Cuba.

Soon cutthroat smugglers would guarantee to "drop off" Cuban refugees within walking distance of U.S. shores. The endeavor was high risk both because of the culpability of the operators and the odds of being detected by authorities in either country. At the least it meant a stay in prison and fines in the U.S. In Cuba, it could mean a life sentence for a convicted smuggler, even for an American citizen. Or it could mean death at sea.

Maria noticed the clouds building in the sky. It looked like there could be bad weather and she wondered if she should be making this trip. She had wanted to write first-hand about the experience from the perspectives of the family, the refugees and the smugglers. She had already interviewed the family in Miami who had sought out Vincent and were paying for his services.

It was another story of a family divided. The sister and her immediate family had come over legally in 1991, soon after the USSR ceased to be an entity and communist funding to Cuba evaporated. The woman's brother however, insisted on remaining with his family and continuing his dissident activities. With Cuba's increased crackdown on dissidents, it was impossible for him to leave legally anymore.

As operators in this kind of endeavor went, Vincent was not as cutthroat as many others. Although he took a fee for his services, his charges were relatively modest, enough to cover his costs. He also had a reputation, so far, for delivering his passengers safely.

He appeared in the doorway of the warehouse. "So," he said, "are you ready for a little boat ride?"

"Are you sure the weather isn't going to be too bad?" asked Maria.

He shrugged. "Good weather, bad weather, I still make the trip."

The boat was an older cigarette boat, but one relatively well maintained. There was a radio and compass, and she noticed some life vests stacked in the corner. As soon as she climbed on board, he started the engine and backed away from the dock.

"Where exactly is the pick-up point?" Maria asked as they left the marina. He pulled out a navigation chart encased in plastic from a shelf at the helm and pointed to a spot near Santa Cruz del Norte. The skies were turning darker. Maria noticed the seagulls flying toward land and she could see whitecaps farther out on the ocean surface.

Halfway across the Florida Straits, it began to rain and both Maria and the pilot put on foul-weather gear. The wind was gusting now and the waves were rising. Maria held on tightly, the rain pelting her face.

As darkness enveloped them, the weather only got worse. The waves were cresting higher and higher and Maria fought a growing sense of panic. Amazingly, though, some three hours after their departure, Vincent announced that they were at their destination just off the Cuban coast. Maria could see nothing to indicate that was the case.

Vincent brought the boat in closer and she could finally barely make out the shoreline. He yelled into his cell phone and within a few moments, six people ran out from under a grove of mangroves into the water, fighting the surf to make their way toward the boat that was now rocking in the waves. As the last refugee was scrambling aboard, a violent wave hit the back of the boat, lifting it into the air and knocking the man back into the water.

Vincent yelled, "Come on! Come on! I can't wait anymore!"

Maria lunged forward and helped pull him into the cockpit while Vincent struggled to maintain control of the craft. Another wave hit, drenching them in seawater and almost tipping the boat over on its side. Vincent revved the engine and turned the vessel away from the shore and back out to sea. They hurtled through the darkness and rain, the refugees struggling into life vests and holding on as best they could.

Maria glanced at the pilot and saw no trace of the confidence he had displayed back at the marina. His face was twisted in fear as he struggled with the wheel.

She yelled to the refugees, "Hold on! Hold on!" as the boat was tossed like a toy between the waves. She saw Vincent was pointing his finger and yelling something, but she couldn't hear what he was saying over the sounds of the waves and the wind and the engine.

Then she turned and saw that another boat was coming directly at them out of the darkness. A huge wave lifted it up over them where it seemed to hang for a moment. Then it came down, crashing upon them, crushing their vessel and plunging them into the water.

The last thing she saw was Dan's face, his eyes looking directly into hers. It was not a dream though. Despite her panic and confusion, she knew they were both part of a nightmare.

# Chapter Nine

Darkness slowly turned to a gray dawn as the crippled *Miguel* lumbered through the waves at a painstakingly slow pace.

The worst of the storm had passed some time ago, although Dan could not remember exactly how long that had been. He held on to the wheel and tried to keep them on a steady course. The autopilot was useless, destroyed by the collision, but the compass still seemed to work. He had put them on a course based on the reverse coordinates from their outward journey. It was the best he could do for the time being. They needed to get out of Cuban waters as soon as possible, something he hoped that had already happened.

Dan's left arm, and especially his ribs, were causing him an increasing amount of pain now. He attributed it to the fall he had taken when he was slammed onto the deck. Maria had disappeared some time ago below decks, trying to help the Cuban doctor treat those who had been injured.

Dan had managed to get the bilge pump below working and it seemed to be keeping up with the leaks, at least for now. Nervously, he scanned the horizon making a full 360-degree turn, but saw nothing except waves that blurred into a horizon where leaden skies met even darker gray waters. There was no land to be seen.

He replayed the scene again in his mind for what seemed like the hundredth time. It was like trying to pinpoint a specific scene on videotape, only to be lost in an endless repetition of forwarding, then reversing the tape. One moment Alberto had been there, and the next he was gone. When was that moment? When had it happened? Had the boats collided once, or was it twice? How long had he blacked out when he hit the deck?

Dan realized that Alberto had stood at this very spot only hours ago. He had held the same wheel as he guided *Miguel* swiftly toward Cuba. Now everything had changed. His friend was gone. He was hurt. The boat was crippled. How many others had they lost?

He could only imagine the force it had taken to break Alberto's strong grip on the wheel and wash him overboard, which is what must have happened, right? How else could he have disappeared? How far off shore had they been? Dan's mind was numb, as he wished his body were, too. It took his full efforts to maintain anything even close to a steady course. Their speed was a fraction of what it had been on the way over, and with only the port engine running, the craft increasingly listed to the starboard side.

With the gray light of dawn upon them, additional dangers faced them. The boat could more easily be spotted and, for that reason anyway, he was glad there was no land to be seen. With the sighting of land came the increased chance of being sighted. He needed to check their exact position on the GPS down below, but couldn't risk leaving the helm, as he struggled with the wheel.

Anger consumed his heart for a moment. Damn you, Alberto! How could you leave me? How could you leave us? How could you let the sea take you? You were always stronger than you looked. Couldn't you have held on a little longer? And why couldn't I find you in the water? With the last question, his anger turned to remorse.

He knew he had to concentrate on saving the boat and its passengers. Dan looked around him and noticed the three other people on the deck, immigrants from the other boat that they had picked up. No one was speaking. Two had blankets over them, but they were soaking wet, and he wondered if the blankets were doing more harm than good. He thought he heard a child crying below as Maria appeared in the hatch and came on deck. Her dark hair was matted and she had a cut on her forehead. She bent forward and spoke quietly with one of the refugees on the deck, then stood and faced Dan.

"How are things below?" he asked.

"We've got some injuries, but none life threatening," she said. "Doctor Mendez is helping those hurt as best he can with the supplies in the first aid kit." She had started to say, "with *Alberto's* first aid kit," but stopped herself.

"Are you okay?" Dan asked. "Your forehead is cut."

"Fine, I'm fine," she said looking absently out at the sea.

"What were you doing out here, Maria?" Dan finally asked.

She turned and looked at Dan directly. "It was a story," she said. "I was doing a story about smuggling immigrants. I had to know about it first hand. I had to know what it was like for the immigrants. And you? Why did you come out with Alberto?"

Dan briefly told the story of Alberto's first mate having been injured. He watched Maria while telling it, and through his raw emotions, it occurred to him how fiercely beautiful she looked. He tried to force himself to focus on the business at hand.

"I'm so sorry all this has happened," said Maria, her voice cracking. "I'm so sorry about Alberto."

"Maria, none of it was your fault," he said, overcoming his concern and sadness. Dan paused, looking out at the rolling seas. He could not imagine what it was going to be like waking up tomorrow and realizing all over again that Alberto was gone. That is, if there was going to be a tomorrow. They still had to figure out a way to make it back to land.

The sound of a plane interrupted his thoughts and instantly brought him back to focus. Dan scanned the skies, but the cloud cover was too low.

"Where is it?" Maria asked. "I can't see it!"

Nor could Dan. He hoped the low ceiling would give them cover. He silently worried that it might be a drug enforcement plane. If that were the case, the Coast Guard would not be far behind. He and Maria continued to peer at the clouds. Eventually, the sound of the droning motor faded. It had flown over and had not circled back.

"Can you take the helm?" he asked Maria. "I need to go below to check the GPS and figure out where we're at. You're going to have to really lean into it. It's pulling hard to starboard."

Maria bravely took the wheel while Dan limped to the ladder, then slowly climbed down into the crowded space below deck. Every step hurt badly. Dr. Mendez looked up and simply nodded as he returned to the task of creating an improvised splint for a woman who must have broken her arm in the course of the collision.

Dan nodded back and carefully worked his way through the small hold, now crowded with injured and frightened people, over to the chart table. He found the shattered remnants of the main GPS unit strewn on the wet floor. It was useless, but then he remembered that Alberto also had a small back-up unit, a hand-held one. He began the search around the compartment, trying to imagine where it might have been stowed.

Suddenly he remembered that Alberto kept it in a cubbyhole under the navigation chart table. It was there and in one piece. He tried activating it, but there was no response. Maybe it's the batteries, he thought. He checked several places, but found none. Helplessly, he gazed around the cabin. He was running out of options and with every increased breath, his already aching ribs hurt more.

The pain served to focus his thoughts. He realized now that he had committed one of the cardinal sins of seamanship: "It is the skipper's responsibility to fix the position of the craft as precisely and as frequently as required." Dan could still recite the rule from the *Chapman Piloting Guide*, but reciting it did not help.

The hours since the collision and the frantic search for survivors seemed to him to have passed in a fog. He remembered initially checking the compass and setting them on the reverse heading. In general terms, he knew that would put them heading back in the direction from which they had come. But he should have been taking a series of interim readings. He still did not know where they were, not exactly anyway, and that would become increasingly important as they neared the Florida coast. He *hoped* they were nearing the Florida coast.

"Your ribs, they are hurt, yes?" Dan felt a hand on his shoulder and he involuntarily flinched. It was Dr. Mendez. "I can see you are in pain," he said. "Let me at least wrap them."

Dan shook his head. "I'm fine. What I really need are a couple of batteries, or maybe a new GPS unit. Do you have any of those?" But the doctor turned away and knelt down again, apparently to again tend to the injured.

Dan knew how well prepared Alberto had always been. He must have kept extra batteries somewhere on board, he thought. But as often happens in situations of stress and panic, his mind turned elsewhere.

An ironic thought came to him. He remembered that the wife of one of his printing clients had purchased a state-of-the-art hand-held GPS unit for her husband that Christmas. It enabled him to pinpoint within a few yards his exact location anywhere on Earth. This was the gift she bestowed upon a man who never journeyed out into the woods or the seas. He would happily track his progress on the short drive to and from work. And here *they* were, somewhere in the

Florida Straits, in a damaged and leaking craft, and helpless to figure out their location.

Then Dan glanced down at the doctor. Amazingly, he saw that the man held four AA batteries cradled in the palm of his hand. Dan looked at him, then at the batteries, suspecting that he might be hallucinating.

"From the flashlight," Dr. Mendez said. "Will your gadget run on Cuban batteries?"

For the first time, Dan felt a glimmer of hope. He fumbled with the back of the GPS unit, dumping the old batteries onto the floor. He tried to keep his breathing shallow to reduce the pain from his ribcage as he bent down to take the new batteries from the outstretched hand. The doctor stepped in to help him, delicately inserting the batteries, then closing the back, and switching it on. Nothing. There was no response.

Patiently, the doctor opened the back again, peered into it closely, pulled out one battery and flipped it end-to-end, then reinserted it. The green screen lit up immediately and Dan grasped the device to read their coordinates. The good news was that Dan now knew where they were. The bad news was that it was far from where they wanted to be.

He could have gotten his coordinates mixed up or the storm might have blown them far off course or the compass could have been damaged. There were any number of ways it could have happened. In any case, they had traveled far to the west instead of north. Dan rechecked the GPS unit in his hand, then rummaged about the table until he found the navigational chart he wanted. Luckily, they were all plastic coated and had been protected from being drenched in the course of the storm and the collision.

He focused on the chart, then sighed. They had wasted a lot of precious time and fuel traveling in a northwesterly direction when they should have been going to the northeast. They were currently at a point far west of the Florida mainland, just south of where the Dry Tortugas extended out into the Gulf of Mexico beyond the Florida Keys.

Dan was thinking that they should soon be able to see land when he heard Maria shouting for him. Instinctively, he bolted for the ladder, but tripped and ran squarely into the counter. The pain was so intense that it brought him down into a heap on the floor without him ever uttering a sound.

Maria was still calling for him when Doctor Mendez appeared at the top of the ladder to tell her that Dan was unconscious. She could only nod and look toward the horizon where another vessel was quickly approaching them.

After Dan had gone below, Maria found it almost impossible to keep the craft on a straight course. Even with all her weight on the wheel, all *Miguel* wanted to do was limp in an endless series of broad circles.

Eventually she found a way to pivot her hips and put her full weight on the wheel so that it no longer took such incredible exertion. It was from this perch that she noticed the small dot on the pale horizon that slowly grew in size, dark and ominous.

Having fixed the location of the oncoming craft in her mind, Maria quickly scanned the horizon in all directions. That's when she noticed what appeared to be land, perhaps low slung islands, just to the northwest. Why hadn't she noticed them before?

The ship was coming from the east and was quickly closing the distance between them. She could now make out that it was not a private craft, but a military ship, probably the Coast Guard.

Maria knew they only had one chance now. She took a deep breath and yelled for everyone on deck to hold on as tightly as possible. Then she pushed the throttle to its full forward position and leaned against the wheel with all her remaining strength. They needed to make landfall before being intercepted.

*Miguel's* one functional engine roared to life with surprising force and the craft immediately picked up speed. It was all Maria could do to keep it aimed on a fairly straight course. Finally, one of the young male Cuban immigrants scrambled from the deck and joined her at the helm.

The Coast Guard vessel had been moving to intercept them, but it now had to change course as it fell in behind *Miguel*. Despite having to alter its course, though, the larger vessel was again quickly closing the distance between them. Maria heard a male voice over a loud hailer ordering her to immediately come about. She concentrated on ignoring those orders, as well as the plumes of smoke that had begun emanating from the engine compartment.

Maria did not back off the throttle, but instead pushed it even harder forward, seeking to get every last ounce of thrust from the failing engine. Now she could clearly see bits of land cropping up from the sea directly ahead of them. She yelled again for everybody to hold on tightly. At the last moment, the Coast Guard vessel backed off before reaching the shallow waters and coral. *Miguel's* shallow hull churned ahead leaving behind a trail of smoke above the waves.

The impact wasn't as bad as she thought it might be as the boat ran aground. There was an awful groaning sound as it came to a halt, then tilted over to one side, lodged in the coral. Clouds of smoke were now pouring out of the engine compartment as everyone started scrambling to get off the boat.

"Get to shore!  Get off the boat and onto land!" she yelled.

Last out of the hold were Dr. Mendez and his son.  They carefully lifted Dan's unconscious body from the cabin.  Maria bent down and stroked his head as they gently put him down on the ground.  They had made landfall, and Maria desperately hoped they were standing on U.S. soil.

# Chapter
Ten

If Maria's Castro article had been widely read and well received in journalistic circles, news of the shipwreck—and the fact she managed to make it back to the U.S. safely with a boat full of Cuban refugees—electrified the news media. Their attention was heightened even more when it was revealed that Dr. Mendez was not just another Cuban doctor, but a well-respected heart specialist, whose departure was acutely and personally embarrassing to Castro.

The story captured headlines in newspapers and television broadcasts across the country: "Reporter Captains Refugee Boat to Freedom" read one headline; "Famous Surgeon Rescued by News Writer" was another; and finally "Wreck at Sea: Reporter Survives to Save Others." The list went on and on.

At the *Herald*, Max Silva was deluged with questions and requests to interview Maria, who had suddenly become as much a celebrity as a journalist.

"No," he said wearily at his second press conference of the day, "Maria Montoro was not authorized to be on either of the boats that picked up the Cuban refugees. The *Herald* does not condone the illegal emigration of refugees from Cuba. Ms. Montoro was working on a story for this paper about those activities, but it was her own decision to accompany the boat captain on the mission."

"Did Ms. Montoro meet Dr. Mendez while she was in Cuba interviewing Castro?"

"No, I thought we'd been over that before," Max said. "Dr. Mendez was on the *other* boat, the one that collided with the one on which Ms. Montoro was a passenger. I don't believe she even knew he was on board until after the collision, when she and the other passengers had been transferred to the boat he and his family were on."

Max paused and looked at the room full of reporters. "I'd like to emphasize one other thing again, too, which is that Ms. Montoro was a journalist researching a story and not an active participant in actually picking up any Cuban immigrants. After the accident, her only goal was to save as many lives as possible, and that involved getting to the U.S. mainland; or in this case, the Dry Tortugas."

"Max, we've received a report that Raúl Castro has issued a statement condemning the episode and accusing Ms. Montoro of being a U.S. spy. Can you confirm or deny this?"

"I won't even give it the dignity of a response," said Max.

"One last question," somebody else shouted. "Where exactly *is* Ms. Montoro at the moment?"

At Memorial Hospital in Miami, Maria sat perched at the foot of Dan's hospital bed as the young doctor walked in with his clipboard.

"So, how are my famous patients doing?" he asked.

Dan tried to smile. "A little tender around the ribs, but fine," he said.

"It's going to take a bit of time, but now that we've got you taped up, I think those three cracked ribs will heal just fine." He paused to look briefly at the bandaged cut on Maria's forehead. "I don't see any reason why you can't be released today," he said.

After Maria had managed to steer *Miguel* onto the reef in the Dry Tortugas, the group had been airlifted to Miami, with Dan and three of the immigrants taken immediately to the hospital. The Cuban immigrants had quickly gone through Immigration and Naturalization Service asylum interviews. It was clear they would all be granted asylum, despite a spate of official protests from Havana.

Since their arrival back in Miami, Maria had kept a low

profile, agreeing to no interviews, and referring all media inquiries to Max at the *Herald*. The cut on her head had required a few stitches, but other than being somewhat bruised and battered, she had managed to survive the ordeal in relatively good shape. It was somewhat of a blessing to her when the hospital had insisted she remain confined, in case her superficial head injuries led to something more serious.

She looked at Dan and realized that their close brush with death at sea, and especially the loss of Alberto, had brought them together in a way neither of them could have anticipated. With the electric moment when they had embraced on the boat, everything had changed. They were now soul mates, and yet, somehow she felt as if they had always been so. Why *was* that, she wondered again?

"You know, you really saved my life," said Dan after the doctor had left. "You saved *all* of our lives. In the end, you're the one who got us to shore. If it weren't for you, all of those people would be back in Cuba, or perhaps at the bottom of the ocean."

"No, you saved all of our lives. I just crashed Alberto's boat into a reef and ruined the last engine it had." She tried to smile.

It was painful for either of them to even say Alberto's name aloud. Their physical wounds had been attended to, but the emotional scars were just beginning to form.

"Tomorrow, can we go to the memorial service together?" asked Maria.

"I don't think I could do it alone," said Dan.

The service was organized by Alberto's families; both his adopted family, the Kendalls, and the family he had rescued from Cuba in a trip not unlike his last one.

Hundreds attended the ceremony at a small church in Little Havana, for Alberto was known and respected in the community for his work long before the recent tragedy made him famous. The news media made much of the event, casting Alberto as a modern-day martyr for the cause of Cuban refugees. The crowd swelled with the curious and those who wanted to honor a man they did not know, but whose bravery and dedication commanded respect, even in death. As much of the crowd as could fit in the church, stood shoulder to shoulder, with the overflow standing in the doorways and spilling out onto the sidewalks. The parking lot was ringed by local television crew trucks with their antennas extended high above the church's steeple for live transmission.

"We haven't seen this kind of a crowd in Little Havana since the Elián Gonzáles episode," said Gina Alexis, a television news reporter. "Although there is no official estimate of the crowd size, we're certainly talking about thousands here today, as opposed to hundreds."

Inside the church, Dan and Maria were surrounded by their respective families and friends. Elena sat in the front bench with them and slid over to sit next to Maria when Dan walked to the podium to give the eulogy for his old friend.

It was the hardest thing he had ever done, and there was not a dry eye in the church by the time he had finished. He began by talking about when he and Alberto had first met and their many shared experiences. He talked about Alberto's quest to bring his family and, eventually, many others to freedom. He talked about Alberto's experience when he first arrived in America and the stranger who had helped him. He also spoke of how Alberto had named each of his boats *Miguel*, after the archangel.

He ended by saying, "I can't explain or understand what happened to Alberto, but I know that he died doing something he felt very deeply about. I will always feel his loss. I also believe there really are those who can see angels among us. There are those who can find great goodness in mankind. My friend Alberto Pascual-Kendall was such a man." He consciously used both his friend's family names, thus honoring the country that gave him safe haven and the one whose suffering inspired his life's mission.

Dan sat down beside Maria again and the choir began to

sing. When they finished, everyone stood and slowly filed out of the crowded church into the parking lot. There was a long motorcade to yet another memorial service, this one at the marina where Alberto had docked *Miguel*. A regatta of boats journeyed out into Biscayne Bay. Dan and Maria stood together at the bow of the lead boat and gently placed a wreath in the waters as the sun set. Hundreds of others tossed flowers into the bay that surrounded the wreath as it slowly floated out to sea.

Initially, the Coast Guard authorities had impounded Alberto's boat, but Dan paid the necessary salvage fees and had it towed back to the marina in Miami where he had it placed in dry dock.

"It's pretty wrecked, you know," said Jared, the best mechanic at the marina.

"I know, but it got us back to shore alive. Jared, I want to fix it; I want to make it as good as it used to be. Can you help me?"

Jared eyed the damaged boat critically, but finally nodded and said, "We can give it a try."

Jared started with the hull, which was badly damaged. Both engines had to be pulled out and replaced as well, and the shafts, drive assemblies, and rudder mechanisms. Dan had all new electronics installed, the very latest technology. He knew Alberto would have appreciated that. Slowly, the boat took shape again. A few weeks later, they were able to put it back in the water. Dan arranged for it to be kept at the same slip where Alberto had moored it.

Dan found himself spending most weekends at the marina, often staying overnight on the boat. Bringing *Miguel* back to life again brought him a certain comfort that eased his mourning for Alberto.

He saw Maria more often now, too. She usually stopped by in the course of the weekend to bring some food, or just to talk and spend time with him. Over the past weeks, they had traded life stories with each other. He learned about her life growing up in Cuba, and she learned what it was like growing up in Miami outside the enclave.

The tragedy they shared had linked them together for life. Their days together at the marina served to heal their troubled souls, and brought them even closer.

They were sitting on the hull as Dan finished adjusting a hatch cover on a Sunday afternoon. He looked across the bay, squinting into the sun, and said, "You know, Maria, there is something we still need to do."

"Hmm?" She looked at him quizzically.

"We have to take *Miguel* out again. It's been ready for a while now. Everything's fixed. It's as good as new, maybe better. I've just, I don't know, I've been putting it off for some reason."

"Well, if you want a first mate, I'm yours," she said smiling as she stood up and brushed off her shorts.

Dan smiled, too, and got up, standing in front of her. He casually pulled a pack of Wrigley's gum out of his pocket and offered her a piece. Maria tilted her head for a moment and stared at him, and then at the outstretched hand.

Instantly, she was transported back to her childhood.

"Hey, are you okay, Maria?" he asked concerned.

"It's just that... I just had the strangest flashback to the day I first arrived here, at the airport, just before Christmas. There was a little boy. I'd never seen him before. He offered me a stick of gum... just like you did. He came out of nowhere, and suddenly, he was right in front of me. He was as close as you are right now."

Dan's blue eyes grew bigger. He looked closely into Maria's face before recalling.

"She was wearing a white dress," he said. "I saw her across the lobby in the terminal. There were so many people, but I couldn't take my eyes off her. She looked so beautiful. And she wasn't afraid. She was... like an angel."

"When I took the gum, he smiled at me. And I promised myself I would never forget the look in his eyes," she said. "I couldn't believe his kindness to a stranger, one who didn't even speak English."

"I've hoped my whole life that I would meet her again someday," Dan said stepping closer and gently pulling Maria toward him.

"Was it really you?" she asked. "Is it possible?"

Dan answered her with a kiss. He kissed her for all the time they had been apart and for all the time they would be together. He kissed her for that moment and for eternity. He kissed her with a passion that he had not known before, but having found it, let his heart run with it, as fast and hard and free as it could.

When their lips parted, Maria looked into his eyes and smiled. "Gracias," she said.

In the early evening, they took the newly reconditioned *Miguel* for its maiden voyage. When Dan started the engines, they turned over easily and came to life with a smooth, low rumble. Maria cast off the last line as Dan slowly eased the boat from the dock. They took their time, leisurely heading out across Biscayne Bay. *Miguel* glided smoothly across the flat waters that reflected a rose-tinted sun setting behind them. Maria stood beside Dan, her dark hair blowing over suntanned shoulders.

"It's going to be a beautiful night," he said. He put his arm casually around her shoulder. It was a good feeling, his arm around her. As the cool evening air blew around them, she felt the warmth and comfort of his touch.

As they crossed Biscayne Bay passing under the MacArthur Causeway and around Dodge Island, Maria asked, "Where are we going?"

Dan smiled and held her closer, but didn't answer. Darkness was coming upon them as they approached Fisher Island. He slowed the boat, halting the engines, and letting it drift briefly. Finally, he dropped anchors from both the bow and stern and secured them.

He turned to Maria and kissed her again, longer this time, and with more passion. When they stopped, she made no effort to pull away, but instead kept her head close to him, her forehead resting on his neck. She breathed in deeply and inhaled his masculine scent mixed with the sea air. She liked it.

And he liked the feeling of her close against him. Their bodies molded together as if they were made for one another. He stroked her hair, his fingers gently brushing her cheek.

Maria turned to look back at the skyline of Miami, and Dan thought she'd never looked more beautiful. In the faint light from the cabin, her skin glowed from an afternoon on the boat, her shoulder-length hair slightly windblown. The stars were coming out now. They stood there for several minutes looking at the skyline before Dan gently pulled away from her saying, "I'll be right back."

He went down below and a moment later she could hear music playing, the melody drifting toward her. Then Dan appeared with a bottle of wine and two glasses. He grinned broadly.

"Look what I found," he said.

"If I didn't know better, I'd say you were trying to romance me," she said smiling.

"I'm glad you don't know better," he said.

Dan reached into his back pocket and produced a corkscrew. He handed the glasses to Maria to hold while he deftly opened the bottle.

"It's Australian," he said. "It's been chilling in the galley cooler all day."

Maria took a sip; it was delicious, not too sweet, not too dry. He raised his glass as she did hers. They clinked their glasses in a toast.

"Well," he said, "here's to old friends."

"And new beginnings," she said, smiling at him.

A little later, Dan put his glass down and took her hand to lead her toward the ladder to go below, but she pulled back.

"No," she said. "Let's stay up here. Bring a blanket."

When Dan returned, Maria was waiting. She stood in front of him. Slowly and gracefully, she disrobed; first the blouse, then the shorts. Then she came to him and unbuttoned his shirt. It slipped off and dropped to the deck.

Now they were touching, his chest against her breasts, his arms around her shoulders, moving down her back in slow circles. Maria caressed him tightly and began to slide down his shorts. Soon his clothes were off, too, and their bodies were wrapped around each other, touching, caressing, kissing. He alternately kissed her lips, then moved to her cheek, then ran his tongue along her neck tracing an unseen path down to her breasts.

They made love under a moonless night that made the stars shine even more brightly. At first their lovemaking was reckless, with the passion of two lost souls reunited. Later, they moved more slowly, carefully drawing out the pleasure for each other as long as possible.

The heat of their bodies contrasted with the cool evening air. The gentle rocking of the waves made *Miguel* sway to and fro. They found the ancient rhythm of the sea and made it their own. The world around them became insignificant as they moved to a different place that was neither sea nor land. With hearts pounding and breath quickening, they melded completely, wrapped around and inside one another.

Afterward, they lay in each other's arms, lost in a timeless place on the other side of ecstasy. They watched the heavens and felt their hearts beat rhythmically together; they listened to each other breathe. Neither one moved, nor could they imagine wanting to be in any other place or time. Maria shifted comfortably in the nook of Dan's arm, resting her head on his chest. They were one.

As they looked up at the stars from the deck of *Miguel*, it seemed like all the heavens revolved around them. Passions spent, they remained at the precise center of a universe shared only between the two of them.

They returned to the marina late that night. Dan quietly eased *Miguel* into its mooring and Maria tied off the lines.

"You're sure you won't spend the night?" he asked.

"I would love to, but I need to get into work tomorrow, early. I wish we could have stayed out there forever," she added.

"Me, too," said Dan.

Although it was late, neither one wanted to leave. Suddenly they were back on land but each secretly yearned to be back on the water, where it was just the two of them, the stars, and the waves. Neither mentioned these thoughts. Instead, they made small talk about schedules and work, and things that at this moment didn't seem to matter to either of them.

Reluctantly, Dan walked her to her car, where they kissed again. In Dan's mind, it felt like a good-bye kiss, and that was the last thing he wanted. Too much had happened between them. He felt like he could never let her go again.

Maria had already started to fumble for her keys, when she stopped and looked into Dan's face.

"This wasn't just about one night, was it? You know..." and she trailed off without finishing the sentence. There were tears in her eyes.

Dan held her by her shoulders, and gently but firmly, pulled her closer to him.

"This is about forever, Maria. I love you. I've always loved you; I just couldn't find you for so long. Now that I have, I will not lose you again."

"Good," she said smiling, "because I'll love you, too, forever."

Maria did not go home that night. Instead, they walked back to the boat, down below in the cocoon of the hold this time.

After quietly making love again, they fell into a deep and sound sleep. When dawn arrived a few hours later, it found them wrapped in each other's arms under covers in the comfortable and protective confines of *Miguel*'s bow, sound asleep.

When the alarm clock went off at 7:00, Dan's arm, perhaps instinctively, reached out from under the sheets to turn it off.

They were both late for work that morning, and neither one regretted it.

# Chapter Eleven

The idea for the book did not happen at once. Instead, it came to her slowly as a result of so many things: their near escape from death in the Florida Straits, the loss of Alberto, and the elation of knowing that she and Dan had finally found one another. The combined effect of all these events made her feel as if she had been on an emotional roller coaster, racing from happiness to great sadness, then back to happiness. The sad regrets that would stay with her always were somehow balanced by the many things she could be thankful for.

It was the photo that finally crystallized it for her. She sat at her desk at the *Herald* on a Monday morning looking at it again. The day after she and Dan had taken *Miguel* out for its "maiden voyage," she had ventured into the record room at the *Herald* searching through the old files. That was where she found it, the photo that had been taken of them so many years before.

The grainy black and white image showed a young boy offering a young girl a stick of gum. The caption under it read: "Hope for the future? An American boy offers a small gift of friendship to a young Cuban immigrant at Miami's International Airport after her arrival. These kids may have something to teach the rest of us about international diplomacy."

Yes, Maria thought, perhaps they did. Maybe it takes a child's heart to overcome years of aggression and distrust between two nations. She looked at the photo of her and Dan and studied their young faces. She saw the hope that comes from kindness. Perhaps it takes the honesty of a child for one to dare to open up enough to reach for peace. Only innocence would allow one to do such a thing, she thought. As we get older, it's easy to become hardened in one's ways and views. We don't start out distrusting, but we learn to. The same way we learn to fear and hate and fight.

War is but an old man's game in which young men die. Who had said that, she wondered? It was true. Adults bear the responsibility to leave the world a better place for their children. Yet they are the ones who wage new wars in which young people die.

All of Maria's journalistic experience told her that many, many people on both sides of the Florida Straits yearned for normalized relations between the United States and Cuba. They were weary of a stalemate that had caused so much pain and sorrow for so long now.

An embargo over four decades old made little sense

anymore as a tool to effect change. Two generations after the embargo, families were still torn apart and some still risked their lives on rafts to be reunited. Two generations after Castro's revolution, people still lived in poverty and pain and hunger. She had walked the streets of Havana and had seen for herself the desperation in the eyes of the Cuban people.

In her soul now filled with passion and hope, she knew nothing *could* change unless the people made it so. The dream of a free and open Cuba could only be possible if the hearts and minds of the Cuban people believed in it enough to make it a reality.

Castro, she knew, would never willingly yield power of his own accord. That was clear in the course of her interview with him. She could never forget the terrible darkness she had seen behind his eyes just before her departure. He was incapable of, or more accurately, unwilling to alter his course. His legacy would be to remain in power at all costs.

And change could not come externally, for the country had been exploited too many times by outsiders. The effort to dominate Cuba, first by Spain, then by the United States, and finally by the Soviets, had left deep scars. That kind of change would not work. The change she imagined would have to come from within Cuba.

But even if change were possible, could it happen in a nonviolent manner? Could there really be a bloodless revolution in Cuba that would finally end the failed policies of communism and open a door to freedom and democracy? Or was this whole notion only a silly dream?

She still remembered Elena chastising her on her 21st birthday.

"You are child if you believe such a thing is possible," Elena had said.

And she remembered her response: "Sometimes it takes the child within us to see new possibilities."

She realized now that these thoughts had been with her for a long time, she simply hadn't assimilated them before. Like seeing only the scattered pieces of a patchwork quilt, the complete design cannot be imagined. It had taken all the events in her life for her to see it clearly in the manner in which she now did.

She thought of Alberto, who had perished in the wreck at sea that night. Perhaps it was meant to be his legacy that the suffering and deaths should finally stop; that a free Cuba should finally emerge from the darkness and shackles of a totalitarian regime.

Now was the time to act. She knew this in her heart. There should be no more lives lost, no more families divided by old policies and entrenched positions. There should be no more souls untethered in a yearning to live in freedom. The ocean floor between Cuba and Florida was already home to too many. The mired political deadlock between Cuba and the United States that had spanned so many years needed to end, now. And it needed to end in a peaceful manner. There had been enough bloodshed, enough tears, and enough wasted lives.

As she sat at her computer, Maria's thoughts spilled out, her fingers found the keyboard, and she started writing. She wrote that day, and the next, and the next. She wrote evenings and weekends and lunch hours. It came to her quickly, with surprising ease, once she began.

As with everything in Maria's life, she was passionate about the project and that passion consumed her. She found she could no more stop writing than breathing. The hours turned into days and then weeks, and she finished it in a flurry. Within two months, the book was done.

As Maria pulled into the marina, she saw Dan standing on the deck of *Miguel*. His ribs fully recovered, he looked trim and athletic. Despite his busy publishing schedule, Dan almost always tried to spend weekends on the boat.

Maria had, of course, told Dan of her writing, and he had waited patiently for her to expend her emotions and energies.

215

He honored her convictions and she, in turn, rewarded him with the ever-increasing love that had blossomed under that starlit night on Biscayne Bay.

The two of them often returned to the bay on Sunday afternoons and just let the boat drift while they read their Sunday papers and made love. Now Dan saw her and smiled as he waved.

"I've brought you something," she said as she came onboard.

Dan looked at the bound typewritten pages in her hands.

"Well, the infamous manuscript. You've finished it *already?*" he said, taking it. "I don't know how you found the time to do it in such a short period of time while still keeping up with all your other work, Maria."

She smiled and shrugged. "It was strange. It was a story that wanted to be told, I guess. Can you read it right now? Do you have time?"

Dan got them each a beer and then he sat out on the sunny deck of *Miguel* with her manuscript. He and Maria had talked about it often, but only in general terms. He hadn't wanted to pry and knew he would see it when she was ready to show it to him. Maria sat cross-legged on the opposite bench watching him behind her sunglasses as he slowly turned the pages.

He said nothing, gave no clue as to his thoughts, as he read. When he finally finished, he closed the manuscript and looked at her in awe.

"It's amazing, Maria. It's really a beautiful story, a child's story, a simple tale, but so much more."

"Gracias," she said and smiled.

"And we're all in it, too. I recognize some of the characters."

"I know," she nodded, somewhat embarrassed. "It was the way I needed to tell the story. It all goes back to what you and I already knew the first time we met."

"What do you mean?" he asked.

"That a small act of kindness can change your life. That an open heart can conquer all. That it's better to love than hate. That in the end, truth really does prevail over lies. We've known those things since we were children; we just have to learn to believe in them again."

"What do you want to do with it now?" he asked, sitting up as he placed the manuscript on the center console.

"Well, I'd like to try to get it published, if you think it's good enough."

"It's more than good enough," Dan said. "As a matter of fact, I'd like to publish it myself," he added, smiling broadly before taking her into his arms.

'Once upon a time, there was a magical island surrounded by clear blue waters, where tall palm trees grew and beautiful music could be heard during the day and the night.'

So begins a seemingly benign tale by first-time author Maria Montoro titled *A Simple Tale of Truth*.

Nothing could be further from the truth.

Although written in the simple and direct prose of a children's book, the author delivers a scathing review of the failed policies of communism and Castro's totalitarian regime. Her fairy tale is of a bright young knight who becomes a dark king. He is paraded to the throne by cheering masses of her little make-believe island based on his promises of freedom for the people. Soon, however, the young knight becomes ensnared in the trappings of his own power. It is a story about power and deception and lies. As the years pass, he insinuates a strange double-speak into their island language: freedom becomes enslavement, wealth becomes poverty, and love becomes hate. The dreams he promised the island people become nightmares when realized, but are still cloaked in lofty terms.

Eventually, the lie is complete. The island becomes a prison and music is heard no more.

Ms. Montoro, better known as a journalist who has written extensively on Latin America, more recently made headline news when she safely piloted a boat filled with Cuban refugees to the Florida shore after a wreck at sea. She puts forth a convincing argument for a free and democratic Cuba, but doesn't pull any punches in also criticizing some U.S. policies, including the embargo that has been in existence since the Eisenhower and Kennedy days of the early 1960s.

The aging king of her imaginary island becomes so self-absorbed that he no longer remembers the promises he made when he came to power, nor can he see the ongoing suffering his policies have caused the islanders to endure. While the people remain poor, some escape to a neighboring kingdom where they find prosperity and freedom. But it is a treacherous divide to reach the land of freedom, and many who attempt it, die in the process.

In the short time since it was published, her fairy tale has found increasing popularity and has been taken to heart by many in the Cuban-American community.

Ultimately, the citizens of the imaginary island find the courage to gather together and cause the departure of the aging and increasingly derelict King. No sword is drawn. It is a peaceful revolution that ends the dark monarchy on the island.

One might call it a fairy tale, but the analogy to the real world is close enough that Fidel Castro, whom Ms. Montoro interviewed earlier this year, personally condemned the book and has outlawed it in Cuba. Copies have been publicly burned. According to Cuban authorities, it is currently considered as contraband, and anyone caught with a copy could face fines and possible imprisonment. Despite this, smuggled copies of it are rumored to continue turning up from Havana to Santiago de Cuba.

The occasions when literary efforts rail against the ills of a society and actually move the populace to action are rare in history. George Orwell's *"Animal Farm"* and Harriet Beecher Stowe's *"Uncle Tom's Cabin"* come to mind.

While this work certainly has people on both sides of the Florida Straits talking, it remains to be seen to what extent life may, in this case, imitate art.

Elena, who had agreed to act as Maria's agent, finished reading aloud the "Books in Brief" section of the *New York Times Book Review* and folded it over. She looked across the table at Maria where they were sitting with Dan in his office and said, "Well, what do you think?"

Maria smiled and said, "It's certainly flattering to get reviewed in the *New York Times*."

"As if that were the only review! Look at all these!" Elena

221

said holding up a stack of clippings. "I'm getting so many requests for interviews that I may have to quit my lobbying business just to manage your personal appearances. Who'd have thought your little book would get all this attention?"

Since Dan had handled the initial printing of the book, much had happened. He and Maria had chosen not to go through regular publishing distribution channels, and instead, all but gave the book away. The message was far more important to them than any potential profit from book sales.

With Elena's help, he and Maria had compiled an extensive mailing list of individuals to whom they had sent copies. In this manner, a word of mouth campaign was mounted and quickly grew. Soon, orders were coming in from around the country. The response was overwhelming. It was now back on the press for its third printing.

"We do have a problem," said Elena. "It seems that the initial shipments to Cuba have all been destroyed, publicly burned on Castro's direct orders. I've even heard he has people literally going door to door in communities searching for copies. He really seems to be taking this very personally," she added, looking directly at Maria.

Maria nodded. "Yes, I imagine he would. It doesn't surprise me."

"I think it's crucial that we get more copies of this book

into Cuba as soon as possible, " said Elena leaning forward. "I know Castro has effectively blocked any traditional means of getting the books into Cuba, despite the fact that people are clamoring for it. I have some contacts who would be willing to act as clandestine couriers to bring copies into Cuba. And I know others, inside Cuba, who are willing to distribute them, despite the consequences."

"We can't ask people to take that risk, Elena," said Dan.

"I thought the whole point is that the needless suffering and dying stop," said Maria.

"We don't have to ask. They are offering of their own free will. They have come to us. Besides," added Elena, "the message has to reach the people if there is any hope for change."

Dan paused as he considered the options. "Okay," he finally said. "If you can set it up on the receiving end, I'll take a shipment of books across the Straits myself in *Miguel*."

"No!" cried Maria. "You're not doing that again, ever."

"I can't ask others to do something I'm not willing to do myself," he said simply.

In her mind Maria knew he was right, but her heart dreaded the thought of either of them crossing the Straits of

Florida on another clandestine mission. The memories of Alberto were far too immediate in her memory, and she simply couldn't bear the thought of losing Dan.

"Loaded stem to stern, I can probably take 5,000 copies in *Miguel*," said Dan, already figuring out the logistics of the trip. "We'd have to carefully choose a rendezvous point, and we would only go for it if the weather conditions were near perfect."

"Fine," said Maria defiantly and with a passion Dan had come to know well, "but you're not going alone."

Castro leaned back in his chair behind the large desk in his ornate office. In the middle of the desk was a small book. Standing uncomfortably in front of him were selected senior members of his cabinet, including the ministers of internal security and the Committee for the Defense of the Revolution. His brother Raúl stood quietly off to the side in the shadows. Castro picked up the book and held it in front of them.

"How many copies of this piece of trash, this *basura,* are still in my country?" he asked tersely, trying hard not to raise his voice. "How many? And where does she find the nerve to call it *A Simple Tale of Truth*? These twisted lies!"

Angrily, he threw the book onto the floor.

"No more than perhaps a handful, *Comandante*," said the interior minister. "All other copies have been collected and publicly burned. I can assure you that any remaining copies will be confiscated within the next few days. We are also closely monitoring all entry points. The populace is aware of its illegality."

"We have also organized demonstrations against the book here in Havana and in Santiago de Cuba," offered the Committee for the Defense of the Revolution minister. "We are looking closely in every community to ensure no one is harboring a copy of it."

"I want the coastal patrols stepped up," said Castro finally. "Since all legal routes are now blocked, I suspect that an attempt may be made to smuggle this garbage into the country. If that should be the case, I want to be personally notified as soon as the perpetrators have been arrested. These lies cannot be allowed to be spread. Does everyone here understand me?"

"Yes, *Comandante*. Absolutely!" said the internal security minister.

"And if anyone is caught hiding or attempting to distribute copies of this book, the strongest penalties will be applied. Is that also understood?"

The cabinet members nodded in agreement and gladly left the office. Alone with his brother, Castro opened the book and absently thumbed through it again.

"We have been betrayed," he mumbled, "by this cursed reporter and her child's tale."

# Chapter Twelve

Pete thought it odd when Dan called him. Since when does the president of a company call a delivery driver to ask a favor? Sure, he'd worked for Dan for almost 15 years now and knew he was a straight shooter; but still, all things considered, it was odd.

Pete found him waiting out back on the warehouse dock late that day as he pulled the truck in from his last delivery. They shook hands and Dan asked about Pete's family.

"We're doing fine. The twin's are nine now and we're finally getting some sleep at night. I reckon that will change in a couple more years when they get into their teens, though." Dan smiled and nodded, but then turned serious.

"Listen, Pete, you're going to have a special delivery on your schedule tomorrow for 5,000 copies of a book." He showed him a slip of paper. "Instead of the warehouse address shown on the delivery sheet, I need you to take them to this marina, and I'll meet you there. Can you make it the last delivery of the day?"

"Yeah, sure, boss," said Pete.

"I know this must seem strange to you, but I wouldn't ask you if it wasn't important. You've trusted me in the past, right?"

Pete nodded seriously. He remembered all too well his brief bout with drugs that nearly cost him his family and his job. He knew that nobody in their right mind would have even considered keeping a high-school dropout who had gotten busted for possession of crack cocaine just two months after hiring in.

Pete was so humiliated at the time that he couldn't bring himself to even call his family from jail. He used his one phone call to dial the work number instead. It was long after hours and he expected to just listen to the phone ring, then shuffle back to his cell. Amazingly however, Dan answered the phone himself on the third ring. Within an hour, Pete was out on bail. The next week, he was into a drug treatment program and, after six months probation, the charges were erased from his record as a first-time offender. He kept his job and Dan paid him through the whole period.

"The fewer people that know about this, the better," said Dan as he discreetly tried to give Pete a hundred-dollar bill. "Use it to do something special for the kids," Dan said.

Pete pushed it back at him and shook Dan's hand again more vigorously.

"It'll be fine, boss," he said. "I'm glad to do *you* a favor for once."

Pete showed up at the marina the next day in the late afternoon. Dan was on board *Miguel*, but climbed off onto the dock as Pete backed up the truck.

"They all go on the boat," said Dan. Together, they unloaded the cartons of books and stowed them below in *Miguel*. With a lot of lifting spurred on by a sense of urgency, they finished within an hour.

"I have a pretty good idea what you're up to, boss," said Pete wiping the sweat from his face. "I think you're one of the best men I've ever known, but I also think this is a crazy thing to do." He paused awkwardly and shoved his hands deep into his pockets. "I'll keep it under my hat just the same."

"I appreciate it, Pete," said Dan. He waved as Pete drove off in the truck before climbing back onto *Miguel*.

Neither noticed the man sitting in the late model Ford parked in the marina lot who had quietly been taking a series of photographs through the telescopic lens of his high-end camera.

Fully loaded with books and fuel tanks topped off, the boat sat heavily in the water, but with the newly installed engines, Dan knew the remodeled craft could easily transport its cargo.

He studied the charts again that night, having decided to take a different route than the last time. Instead of journeying directly to Cuba, he and Maria would first cross to the Bahamas, to Andros Island, and spend a night there before going to the coast of Cuba. If anyone were watching, it would have the appearance of a casual weekend outing to the Bahamas. The final rendezvous point had been prearranged: a small marina on the northeastern coast of Cuba near Puerto Padre, not far from Las Tunas.

Dan put away the navigational charts and silently regretted agreeing to let Maria come along. She had quickly become an accomplished first mate, but he dreaded the thought of any possible harm coming to her. Even though every detail had been studied and planned and reviewed, there were still risks. There are always risks, he knew.

Maria arrived early in the morning, bright and chipper, despite little sleep. They had both made excuses at work to take off that Friday, telling friends they would be away for a long weekend. With *Miguel* fully loaded, there had been no room to sleep on board, so Dan had stayed the night at his own apartment, arriving back at the marina shortly before Maria.

"You look great," he said handing her a hot cup of coffee he had picked up on his way. "I saw you on Larry King last night."

She smiled and kissed him. "It was a long day. I didn't get back in town until after midnight. Say, look at all these books!" she exclaimed peeking down below where the cartons had been stacked from floor to ceiling.

Balancing his coffee cup in one hand, Dan wedged himself between two stacks of boxes. He turned on the radio and tuned it into the weather band. The latest report confirmed that the weather conditions were near perfect for the trip, flat seas and a gentle northeast breeze.

It didn't take long for them to get under way. They worked with the familiarity of having done this many times before. Dan backed *Miguel* away from the dock and they headed out across Biscayne Bay. Maria stood beside Dan as he piloted *Miguel* and they enjoyed the view of a promising horizon with the sun reflecting on the waters. Back at the marina, the man with the camera kept shooting photos of them until they were far out in the bay before he, too, finally left.

They made the crossing to the Bahamas in a leisurely manner, approaching Andros Island in the early afternoon. Dan could see the low-slung mounds of land as they rose barely above the horizon line. Many of the 700 or so islands that make up the Bahamas are so flat as to be almost invisible until one is almost on top of them.

As they approached land, gulls flew overhead and a group of dolphins swam out to meet them. They circled the boat, cresting above the waves, then plunged down again in a seemingly orchestrated dance that made Maria laugh.

They docked at Behring Point and spent the afternoon snorkeling. In the early evening they went ashore for a light dinner at a little restaurant, not much more than a shack, run by a giant black Bahamian with the unlikely name of Little Joe. He always caught his own fish. Spiced with jerk seasonings, it made for a memorable meal.

"This is so lovely," said Maria. "I wish we could stay longer."

"You come back tomorrow night and I will make you my special conch dish," said Little Joe. "I promise, you will love it."

"We'll be here," they both said laughing.

Back on the boat after dinner, it was all business. Dan tuned the short wave radio to the predesignated frequency and waited. Shortly after the agreed upon time of 9:00 p.m., the radio crackled to life. They had devised a code to deliver the message as quickly and discreetly as possible. There was no verbal communication, just a short series of clicks. In case anyone was monitoring the frequency, it would sound like so much static to the casual, or not so casual, listener.

Dan concentrated intently. It was a go. He quickly keyed the microphone with a series of clicks in response. They would meet at the rendezvous point shortly after midnight. Through Elena's contacts in the Cuban underground, Dan had been instructed as to a specific approach to the island that would enable him to avoid any Cuban Border Patrol boats.

He carefully put *Miguel* on the prescribed course across the Great Bahamas Bank under a half-moon in the cloudless night.

When they were within a mile of the shoreline of Cuba, Dan switched off the running lights on *Miguel*. He had already entered the precise coordinates of the rendezvous point in the very latest GPS unit available that he had installed beside the wheel at the helm. Overlaid on a navigational grid of the immediate area, was a slowly moving dot indicating *Miguel's* position. Another steady dot indicated the rendezvous point. Slowly, the points were converging. The seas were calm and the ride was smooth. At a quarter-mile out another short exchange of clicks indicated that their arrival party was in position and waiting for them.

Dan slowly approached a small dimly lit marina. Maria was the first to spot the narrow flashlight beam flickering at the dock. He eased *Miguel* to the dock as Maria tossed the forward line to waiting hands. When Dan switched off the engine, there was silence except for a gentle breeze blowing through the palms as the other lines were secured.

A smiling young Cuban male dressed in worn fatigues introduced himself as Mario. Dan shook hands with him and introduced Maria. Mario smiled even more broadly and kissed Maria's hand saying, "So, you are the famous author of this book. I am honored to help make sure your words are read by the Cuban people."

With that, Mario quickly directed his four comrades to start unloading the boxed cartons of books. They formed a kind of bucket brigade, with Dan down below handing up the books one box at a time, and each man in turn handing the carton to the next, where Mario stacked them on the dock. They made quick work of it. Within half an hour all the cases were stacked on the dock and *Miguel*, now empty, rested a good deal higher in the water.

Wiping the sweat from his forehead, Dan finally felt he could relax a bit. Everything had worked out exactly as planned. He looked forward to the smooth crossing back to the Bahamas and a couple days of relaxing with Maria, just the two of them. As he climbed up from below, he heard the rumble of a truck engine and saw one of Mario's men backing up an ancient box truck into which Dan assumed they would soon be loading the stacked cartons of books. He didn't know the details as to how the books would be distributed, but knew that through Elena, it had all been worked out.

He vaguely registered the sound of another engine in the distance, but dismissed it, concentrating on the final preparations to depart. Then he turned toward Maria and saw by the look on her face that she had heard it, too. The engine sounds quickly grew louder. Suddenly three jeeps pulled into the marina. In addition to their headlights, they were equipped with spotlights that now bathed the dock in a glaring brightness, temporarily blinding Dan and Maria. There was much commotion and harsh shouts in Spanish.

A canvas-topped flatbed truck pulled to a stop and suddenly the marina was flooded with Cuban soldiers carrying rifles and wearing fatigues. Unlike the ones Mario and his men wore, these were fresh and relatively new. For a fleeting moment, Dan considered making a run for it, but with his eyes now adjusted to the lights, he could see that several rifles were pointed directly at him and Maria, who stood silently beside him. The soldiers ordered Mario and his men to lie prone on the ground and quickly handcuffed them.

One soldier, clearly in command of the newly arrived troops, instructed Dan and Maria in Spanish to get off the boat with their hands above their heads. They were also handcuffed while two soldiers went on board *Miguel* and quickly searched it. Emerging from below deck, one shouted something to the lead soldier who nodded his head as he came over directly in front of Maria.

"We've been expecting you, Señora Montoro. My name is Lieutenant Ambarco, and you and your companions are hereby under arrest for espionage and attempting to smuggle prohibited materials into Cuba."

One of the soldiers grabbed Dan's shoulder and pushed him toward where Mario and his men lay by the flatbed truck. Two other soldiers stood on either side of Maria while the lieutenant talked into a hand-held radio. Dan wished his Spanish were better, as he was having a hard time following the rapid conversation. Maria, however, had no such problem.

The lieutenant was being patched through to command headquarters in Havana.

"We have taken prisoners and confiscated all contraband books. Yes, she is one of them. They arrived as we had been informed and the operation went as planned. Yes sir. I will wait." Maria watched his face and saw him suddenly stand more erect, almost jerking to attention, as he said, "Yes *el Comandante*! We have her in custody at this very moment. Yes sir, we are enroute to Havana immediately."

Even if Maria had not spoken Spanish, she knew there was only person in Cuba with that title.

Dan had caught the words, as well, and saw the look of fear in Maria's face and demanded of the leader, "What's going on, here? Tell me!"

"Silence!" one of the soldiers shouted and leveled the barrel of his rifle at Dan.

Mario, standing next to Dan, tersely whispered, "They're taking Maria to Havana on orders from Castro."

The lieutenant walked purposely toward one of the jeeps, leading the two soldiers who had Maria in their grasp. Dan, along with Mario and the others who had been dragged to their feet, were ordered into the back of the army truck.

Several soldiers now assembled on the dock. There was some discussion among them and Dan saw that two of them were hauling out cans of gasoline. As best Dan could determine, they were discussing how to ignite both the cases of books and the boat. Then, out of the corner of his eye, he saw that Maria was resisting being pushed into the jeep. She had twisted away from the grip of one of the soldiers. The other soldier drew his arm back and slapped her hard across the face, causing her to fall to the ground

"No, you bastards!" yelled Dan. In that instant, rage so filled his mind that he could barely see. But he had seen enough. Clenching his shackled hands together, he interlaced his fingers tightly so the handcuffs became a metal bludgeon around his wrists. Then he swung around quickly and with all his strength struck the closest soldier in the jaw. He followed through as if hitting a ball deep into left field with an imaginary bat. The soldier gave out a grunt as he reeled

239

backwards onto the ground. A few feet away, another soldier yelled and quickly brought up his rifle.

Without hesitating, Dan leaped off the truck and lunged forward, hoping to get to the soldier before he could shoot. Too late, he thought, as he heard the shot and waited to feel the bullet slam into his chest.

But the soldier had not shot. Instead, he toppled to the ground and Dan landed on top of him. As Dan rolled off, he saw the growing blood stain on front of the soldier's uniform. In disbelief, he heard other explosions and watched as another soldier dropped, then another, both with telltale blossoms of red spreading across their chests. Now gunshots seemed to be coming from all over, and chaos engulfed the scene as a firefight ensued between the soldiers and an unseen group of attackers.

Dan tried to locate Maria. The soldier who had hit her was now roughly trying to get her into the back of the jeep. Dan ran into him at full speed, lowering his shoulder, like an offensive lineman taking out an unsuspecting linebacker. He slammed solidly into the soldier's back and took him down.

The lieutenant in the front seat had his pistol drawn and was shouting as the driver fired up the jeep and jammed it in gear. The wheels were throwing dirt as Maria jumped to the side and landed on the ground beside Dan. A moment later, a hail of bullets greeted the speeding jeep. The lieutenant crumpled backwards in the seat, his revolver flying from his hand. The lifeless body of the driver hunched forward over the steering wheel as it veered, crashing into a small building at full speed, its engine still revving wildly.

Crouching beside Maria, Dan saw that one of the soldiers who had been inspecting the boat had managed to avoid being shot. He had picked up the gasoline can and was preparing to heave it toward the dock where the cartons of books were stacked. The soldier swung his arm back and was about to douse the books with fuel when a bullet pierced the can and it exploded. In an instant he was engulfed in a fiery inferno. The explosion was still far enough away not to ignite the books or threaten the boat, but the flames were so hot that Dan and Maria had to retreat.

The shooting stopped as suddenly as it began. Kneeling beside Maria, their hands still shackled, Dan squinted to see through the smoke and darkness. He looked across at the back of the truck and saw Mario move. He hoped that the men were okay.

Other sounds engulfed them. He heard boots shuffling, people running, and terse commands being given in Spanish. Then he picked out an amazingly familiar voice. It came to him as if from across a deep void, as if from another life.

"Hey amigo," it said. "Stand up. Are you okay?"

Shakily, Dan got up. He found himself looking into the face of a dead man. Standing in front of him, dirty and bearded, but still flashing the broad smile he could never forget, was Alberto.

Dan could not find the words. "How... ?" he started to ask. Maria needed no words. She ran to Alberto and threw her shackled hands over his head. She hugged him tightly with tears streaming down her face. Alberto laughed and said, "Hey, hey! Let's get these handcuffs off so you can hug me properly."

More members of the rebel group now came out of the darkness and gathered around them. Alberto uncuffed Dan, who also hugged him fiercely.

"I can't believe you're alive," said Dan shaking his head. "You *are* alive, right?"

Alberto smiled. "No angel; it's me in the flesh."

"But the storm... We thought you'd drowned." Dan's voice trailed off.

"I'll tell you all about it as soon as we get away from here," said Alberto. "Right now we need to get moving before we have more visitors. *El Comandante* is not going to be happy when he learns that his carefully laid trap has failed."

The other rebels were already busily uncuffing Mario and his men before loading the stacked cartons of books into a truck. Alberto paused when he looked at *Miguel* and stared appreciatively at it for a moment.

"If I didn't know better, I'd say that looks like a brand new version of my old boat," he said. "We'll need to get it out of here, too."

"It's your boat," said Dan with a grin. "You move it." He tossed the keys to Alberto who caught them easily.

Then he stopped and listened closely. They all heard the distinctive sound of a military helicopter in the distance, its blades thwacking out a cadence that grew louder by the moment. The rebel soldiers finished loading the books onto the truck and pulled rapidly away, lights extinguished, and disappeared down the jungle road into the night.

Alberto jumped onto the boat with Dan and Maria close behind. They quickly untied the lines as Alberto turned the key and the powerful engines came to life.

He backed away from the dock with practiced speed, then opened the throttle as they sped away from the marina. They ran at nearly full throttle with no lights on for several minutes, the sounds of the helicopter fading behind them. Dan could tell Alberto was enjoying the improved performance of the boat as it fairly skimmed across the water. He could see Alberto's face in the glow of the instrument lights and he marveled that his old friend was alive and once more at the helm of *Miguel*.

They had been traveling for some time along a coastline thick with impenetrable mangroves when Alberto suddenly slowed the boat, then turned directly into the mangrove thicket. Dan and Maria instinctively ducked, but were surprised to see that an apparently solid intertwined wall of brush actually gave way to a low arched opening.

Alberto slowly guided *Miguel* into the heart of the thicket that surrounded them on all sides. A low ceiling of entangled branches allowed only narrow slits of moonlight to shine through. Finally Alberto turned off the motors and let the boat drift slowly forward. With its powerful engines silenced, Dan and Maria could hear vague human sounds amidst the chirping of crickets, the shifting branches in the breeze, and the hooting of an occasional owl. As her eyes adjusted to the intense darkness, Maria noticed the sheltered glow of a small campfire in the distance across the swamp.

Two figures emerged to greet them at the end of the small man-made canal that had painstakingly been cut through the dense mangroves. As they came closer, Dan and Maria could see the silhouettes of a woman and a young girl.

"Welcome to Camp Liberty," said Alberto. "I want you to meet my family."

In the darkness of the collision, the wave had hit Alberto like a solid wall, its force so strong that it literally tore his hands from the wheel. And then there was only darkness. No air, only churning water. He couldn't breathe. He couldn't see. He was so disoriented that he couldn't even tell up from down. His lungs felt like they would burst. His eyes were burning. He craved air. Desperately, he exhaled and let his body's buoyancy lift him toward the surface.

He broke the surface gasping and sucking for air in the middle of a maelstrom. Sheets of rain were coming down. A wave crashed over him and suddenly he was underwater again. He fought back now desperately to the surface, coughing and choking, his eyes and throat burning from the salt water.

At first, the boat was nowhere in sight. Had it sunk? No, he could just make out its form in the darkness, a small dark shape moving away from him in the stormy seas. He tried to yell to them, but to no avail. Suddenly, he glimpsed another person several yards from him. It was a man, thrashing, then disappearing under a wave. Alberto swam toward him as quickly as he could.

When he got to where he thought he had seen him, Alberto sucked in as much air as he could and dove underwater. In the dark waters, he could barely see his own hands in front of his face. Then something grabbed him from behind. The man was frantically pulling him, thrashing about, trying to get back to the surface. The panicked man kept pushing Alberto deeper under water, until Alberto finally managed to disentangle himself and resurface. The man emerged again a few feet away, but was still thrashing about and clearly tiring. Alberto maneuvered behind him in the classic lifeguard position with his arm under the man's chin.

"Do not fight me or we will both die! Do you understand?" he shouted over the storm into the man's ear. The man nodded and relaxed slightly, but still tried to cling to Alberto. Another wave crested over them and the man started kicking and thrashing again. Alberto tightened his grip and the man quickly stopped.

Alberto knew there was no hope of catching up with the boat. It had disappeared into the darkness and rain. Although he was a strong swimmer, Alberto could feel himself fatiguing. He fought back his own feeling of panic. He had to figure out where land was and how far. He forced himself to try to recall their position when the collision had occurred. Perhaps a mile he thought, no more. Could he make it? He could feel the adrenaline pumping through his fatigued body. He would have to make it!

Through a brief lessening of the squall, he thought he could just make out the outline of the darkened coast in the distance. Slowly, doing a modified sidestroke while towing the man, Alberto tried to make his way toward land.

He barely remembered making it to the beach. It seemed like an endless battle between him and the ocean. Several times he was sure he would not be able to go on and that the sea would claim him. The man had stopped all movement some time ago. Alberto worried he may well have passed out or perhaps even drowned, but he clung to him tightly, reflexively. Finally, when he could expend no more effort, Alberto let the waves carry them. He coughed as he inadvertently kept swallowing water and drifted in and out of a daze hoping that the waves would wash them ashore.

The ocean, however, was not so forgiving. A large wave swelled and lifted them, then crested, pushing them forward in a frothy fury. Alberto clutched the man tightly, trying not to lose his grip. Then the wave slammed down forcefully over them, and Alberto lost his grip. Exhausted, Alberto knew this could well be it. So, this is how it ends, he thought. He was resigned to greet the darkness below, but instead Alberto's face was pushed into a sandy floor beneath the water. He found he could touch bottom and he crawled to the beach.

Coughing and gasping, and barely able to stand himself, Alberto saw the limp body of the man a few feet away on the beach, the waves washing over him. He struggled to his feet and managed to drag the man up onto the beach before collapsing on top of him. The ocean would claim no more victims this night.

A woman's voice woke him up. He did not know whether it was day or night, but he was no longer on the beach. He found himself on a cot in a tent. He tried to move, but every muscle in his body begged for him to remain motionless.

"You're lucky we found you when we did," she said. "They stepped up the patrols as soon as the storm subsided. They would have found you for sure."

Alberto tried to focus. She was a dark-haired woman dressed in old tattered fatigues. She was thin and of medium height. Her high cheekbones defined her face and framed dark eyes filled with concern and determination.

"What happened," he asked. "There was a man... did he make it?"

She nodded. "Yes, amazingly. You saved his life."

"Who are you?" Alberto asked. "Where am I?"

"My name is Elsa. My friends call me Elsita. I am a fighter in the resistance movement. We found you on the beach. We were the ones who brought Dr. Mendez and his family to the coast."

"There was another boat," said Alberto weakly. "There was a wreck."

"I know," she said. "We watched from the shore. It was a terrible accident. There has been no word if they made it."

A little girl appeared in the doorway of the tent and peered in shyly.

"My daughter," she said. "Julita, could you please bring me a canteen with water?"

"Your husband? Her father?" Alberto asked feeling increasingly dizzy.

Elsita shook her head. "He was killed by government troops when Julita was still a baby."

"I'm sorry," said Alberto.

Elsita nodded and cradled his head as she brought the canteen up to his lips. "If they find out that there were any survivors from the shipwreck, there will be more search parties, and we cannot afford for our camp to be discovered. Castro will see Dr. Mendez's defection as a personal affront to him. For now, no one must know that you or the other survivor are alive and in Cuba."

Alberto nodded and rested his head back on the cot. Suddenly he felt more exhausted than he ever had before. He slipped off into a deep sleep wondering if and when he would ever return to America. He thought of the beautiful resistance fighter who had found him on the beach and now held his head. He hoped she would be there when he awoke.

Alberto stepped off the boat. In the shadows of the mangroves, the little girl ran to him and hugged him.

"This is my adopted daughter, Julita," he said as he picked her up. "And this is Elsa, my wife. We were just married a month ago." He smiled almost shyly at Dan and Maria. "She was the one who found me washed up on the beach. I would not be alive today if it weren't for her. She was my angel that day, and I decided I did not want to let her go."

"Please call me Elsita," she said shaking hands with Dan and then Maria. "I have read your book," Elsita said to Maria. "And I hope everyone in Cuba can read it soon."

Dan saw that several tents had been pitched under the trees around the small campfire. A few men were gathered off to the side talking in low tones. Alberto introduced Dan and Maria to them before settling by the fire. Elsita offered cups of hot coffee, which Dan and Maria took gladly.

"Thanks for saving us," said Dan. "By the way, you had a heck of a funeral in Little Havana."

"I'm sorry I couldn't get word to you before. It was too risky, and I figured you'd risk your life trying to come back for me. Besides," he added smiling at Elsita, "I found reasons to stay here for a time."

"Are you settling here permanently?" asked Maria.

Alberto shook his head. "No," he said. "It's becoming increasingly dangerous. I was committed to change in Cuba at all costs. That's why I joined Elsita in the resistance movement. But change at all costs can be a very risky proposition. Many lives have been lost already. I worry about Elsita and Julita. I wanted to bring them to America, but Elsita could not abandon the cause."

"When we read your book," said Elsita, "it changed everything. Suddenly we saw the possibility to rally the people for real change in Cuba without bloodshed. We decided to stay long enough to ensure copies of your book reached the Cuban people."

"The truck made it to the distribution point," said one of the men as he emerged from a tent. "Word has just come in on the radio. Copies will be in Santiago and Havana by morning."

"Then it's done," said Alberto looking at Elsita who nodded resolutely.

"We have done what we can. The people of Cuba will soon have in their hands a child's tale that speaks only the truth. We will make the crossing with you tonight. We need to break camp, and the others need to disperse quickly. This entire area will be crawling with Castro's troops once he discovers what has occurred. No good can come from further death and suffering."

Alberto and Elsita went over to confer with the other men. Brief but genuine good-byes were said. Then they went quickly about the business of breaking camp.

When the phone rang at Castro's apartment, he answered it himself. There was a long pause before he spoke.

"This cannot be so!" he said tersely into the phone. "All copies of the book must be recaptured and destroyed. The perpetrators must be found and captured. They cannot be allowed to return to the United States. If necessary, sink the boat. There will be no excuses this time. I want whatever forces necessary ordered into action to accomplish this. All will be held accountable. It will be done at all costs."

He did not slam the phone down when he finished, but placed it back on the receiver with a deadly calm. On the table beside the phone was a stack of color enlargements. The top one was a close-up taken of Dan and Maria as they had left the marina in *Miguel* the previous morning.

The fire was doused and the tents were gone. Elsita quickly gathered what few possessions she and Julita would take with them and put them on board the boat. The remaining resistance fighters piled into a jeep and roared off.

Although still dark, it would not remain so for long.

"We have radio intercepts of troop and Border Patrol movements," said Alberto as he came striding over to them.

"Where?" asked Dan.

"Everywhere," said Alberto grimly. "It looks like Castro is sending not only an army, but also his air force and navy this way. We need to get moving, *now!*"

With Maria, Elsita and Julita on board, Alberto fired up *Miguel's* engines and carefully backed the boat out of the mangrove tunnel while Dan checked the navigation instruments. Once out in open water, Alberto opened up the throttle and *Miguel* lurched forward as a gray dawn slowly lit the skies.

Dan scanned the horizon as they moved away from the Cuban coast. He could see nothing unusual and the roar of *Miguel's* engines drowned out any other sounds. Elsita held Julita in her arms as the wind buffeted them. Maria also nervously watched the horizon and the skies.

"I'm going below to check the radar," said Dan. Alberto nodded from the wheel as he made a slight course adjustment, still actively keeping a lookout.

In the course of rebuilding *Miguel*, Dan had installed the latest radar equipment. He switched it on now, cautious not to leave it on so long as to open them up to detection. He scrutinized the screen for a few moments. There were numerous blips along the coast on the large-scale map, with a small cluster at the marina location that had been their rendezvous point. He guessed they were patrol boats. Two of them had separated from the group and were heading toward them. They had clearly left the camp not a moment too soon. He switched off the radar and silently wondered if they had already been detected.

Back up on deck, Dan had to fairly shout the information for Alberto to hear him. "The marina has a lot of activity right now. Two patrol boats look like they're heading toward us. They're about four miles out, but closing."

Maria trained her binoculars in the general direction that Dan had indicated but could see nothing.

"Most of the Cuban Border Patrol boats are old and outdated," said Alberto. "They'd never catch us. But I've heard rumors that they have a couple newer ones. I've heard they're very fast."

Alberto made another course correction, angling slightly more to the northeast and he opened the throttle. He and Dan both knew it was dangerous to run it at 100 percent for more than extremely brief periods.

Suddenly Maria lowered the binoculars and yelled, "I see one!" She pointed to a spot on the horizon far off their starboard. Without binoculars, Dan and Alberto could not make it out. Alberto checked the GPS unit beside the wheel.

"We're within a few miles of international waters," he said. "They should turn back then. They have no authority beyond that limit."

Dan returned to the radar and kept it on this time, as they had obviously been detected. He zoomed to the close-up screen that showed a two-mile radius around their vessel. He could clearly see the blips indicating the patrol boats. They would never catch up to them inside Cuban waters.

When *Miguel* crossed into international waters, Alberto reluctantly let up on the throttle while eyeing the temperature gauges. One of the engines was running hot. If the temperature didn't drop, he'd have to shut it down, leaving them with only a portion of the power they might need.

Dan studied the radar screen. The blips continued on their respective courses. They were not slowing down or turning back. Dan wondered what orders had been given to them. He opened a compartment and took out a rifle before heading back up. He knew they stood little chance against the guns of a Cuban patrol boat, but it was all they had.

Now they could clearly see the patrol boats on the horizon. They were coming toward *Miguel* from two different directions angling toward each other. The X where their paths would intersect was *Miguel's* location. Dan glanced at Alberto who looked worried.

"Elsita, could you please take Julita down below and monitor the radio frequencies. They may try to hail us," said Alberto. "Maria, you should go down below, too," he added in an even tone, but one that left no room for debate. They were quiet orders from a man who was again captain of his boat.

Dan carefully placed the loaded rifle on the bench and looked through the binoculars. He focused on the approaching boats as they splashed through the waves at what appeared to be top speed. He glanced over Alberto's shoulder at the GPS unit.

"This is crazy. We're clearly in international waters. They should have turned back," said Dan.

Just then the radio crackled to life and Maria turned up the volume. In Spanish, a male voice repeated the command. "You are ordered to come about immediately." Alberto quickly handed the wheel over to Dan and went below.

"We are a United States vessel in international waters," said Alberto into the microphone. "You have no authority to stop or harm us. We demand that you cease and desist threatening activities."

There was only a short pause before the response. "You are under arrest for smuggling and for engaging in subversive activities within the country of Cuba and your vessel is hereby impounded."

Dan heard the burst of fire from the twin machine guns and saw the splashes off the starboard side of *Miguel*. It had been off the mark, but not *that* much.

"Jesus," he said aloud and abruptly changed course, now moving into a random zigzag pattern in an effort to make it difficult to aim at them and establish the correct lead upon firing.

"We will not be boarded. That is final," said Alberto resolutely as he put the microphone back on the radio set and scrambled back up on deck.

The two patrol boats that split off from the rest of the naval vessels converging at the marina were indeed the fastest and most modern in the Cuban Border Guard fleet. As opposed to the heavy and lethargic Soviet-built Zhuk-class vessels, these were much swifter, but equally as lethal.

A carefully chosen Cuban naval officer commanded each. To be given such an honor meant one was clearly a rising star or had already achieved great accomplishments for the cause of the revolution and was thus rewarded near the end of one's career. Such was the case of the two captains who could not have been more different from one another.

At the helm of the first Cuban patrol vessel was Carlos Rimus. At just 22 years old, he had graduated first in his class from the Cuban Naval Academy. He was one of the youngest officers in the Border Guard that consisted of some 6,500 troops. Bright and articulate, he was a natural leader and had quickly advanced through the ranks.

Orlando Aguero commanded the other boat and had been in the Cuban Border Guard for more than 20 years. He had been instrumental in any number of drug interdictions and attempts to land subversives on the shores of Cuba. His allegiance was unquestioned. His performance, given the state of the equipment he had been delegated, was noteworthy. Naturally, he took a good number of bribes, but this was expected, so long as it did not outwardly interfere with official government policy, or more importantly, embarrass *el Comandante* in any way. Embarrassment was a crime not easily forgiven by Castro.

Both captains had received the same orders on their radios, patched through directly from the highest authorities in the Ministry of Interior: They were to pursue the American boat and capture it, or sink it if necessary.

Now Carlos was on his radio to the older Cuban captain. "What are you doing firing at them? We can easily capture this vessel."

"Apparently your interpretation of the orders is not the same as mine," said Orlando.

"What the hell are you talking about? We have the same orders. I heard them as clearly as you did. To capture them is the first option, and it is achievable," Carlos said urgently into his microphone. "There is no reason to do this!"

"As the senior officer in this operation, I am taking the lead," the older officer said. "The decision is mine. Pull back and await further instructions. Over and out."

In the silence that followed, the young captain watched through his binoculars as the other Border Patrol boat adjusted its turret, zeroing in on the American boat.

Dan squinted through the telescopic sight on the rifle as he leveled it at the approaching Cuban boat. For the second time in his life he found himself aiming a loaded gun at another person. Through the sight, he clearly saw the twin guns swivel around and point toward them.

"Good God, they're going to fire at us again!" he yelled to Alberto who was at the helm.

"Brace yourself," shouted Alberto as he jammed the throttle forward to full speed and turned the wheel hard. *Miguel* reacted instantly, powerfully swerving to the left as the guns when off and another burst of fire splashed off their starboard side.

The temperature gauge on the right engine was off the dial and Alberto could hear a high-pitched whining sound coming from the engine compartment. He had no choice, and reluctantly shut down the right engine. At half-power, he knew they would be a much easier target. He turned to Dan.

"You know what you have to do. Take out that captain," he said, "Do it now."

Dan steadied the rifle and aimed toward the bridge of the Cuban vessel. Through the sight, he could clearly see a middle-aged man in his forties wearing sunglasses and officer's markings on his light green Cuban Border Patrol uniform. There was no more time to think. In moments they could be dead at this captain's command. It had come down to him or them. Someone would have to die.

Dan took a deep breath and held it while he slowly squeezed the trigger. In that instant the gun turret on the front of the patrol boat suddenly exploded into flames.

Alberto turned and looked at Dan incredulously, and then at the patrol boat.

"What the hell?" he asked.

Dan stood up. There was another burst of fire and another explosion. The rear area of the approaching patrol boat disappeared into flames and smoke. In a sudden unexpected duel, one Cuban patrol boat had just fired upon the other, clearly disabling it. Maria and Elsita came up on deck and all stood watching the spectacle, open-mouthed.

The radio on *Miguel* suddenly crackled to life with the voice of a young Spanish-speaking male.

"Attention American vessel *Miguel*. This is Captain Carlos Rimus of the Cuban Border Patrol. I am hereby announcing our intention to defect to the United States. On my orders, my men have disabled the weapon and navigation systems of the patrol boat that was about to attack you. If it shows evidence of any other aggressive actions, we will sink it. Any of my crewmembers who do not wish to defect but return to Cuba, may board the other vessel. I have radioed the authorities in Cuba, and they have no doubt already sent escort vessels. Myself and my remaining crew will be happy to escort your vessel and the esteemed author, Ms. Montoro, to U.S. waters."

The young captain placed the microphone back firmly on its clasp. Resting beside the radio at the helm was a children's book, its pages dog-eared from having been passed on from one reader to the next and the next.

He stormed across his office, barely able to control himself. He shouted at an increasingly fearful cadre of aides to get various officials and officers on the phone or to his office immediately. There would be very serious consequences for the incompetence that created this pathetic situation. Appropriate punishment would be meted out in due course, but it would bring him little satisfaction. What he needed now was to solve two serious problems.

Finally settling at his desk, Castro tried to calm himself and again review the situation in his mind. Unknown numbers of the treacherous book were no doubt already being stealthily smuggled across his country. It should never have happened. His surveillance team had acquired the correct information of when and where the books would be smuggled in, and even by whom. They had even provided photos of the boat as it was being loaded.

It should have been a simple operation. His troops had been in place. They had watched the perpetrators arrive, meet their contacts, and unload their subversive materials. His troops had arrested them, only to be counterattacked by a motley gang of rebels. The books should have been burned by now and the journalist should have been on her way to Havana. That was a problem, but not the largest one.

Of the two most advanced patrol boats he had dispatched to apprehend them at sea, incredibly, one had been crippled by the other. Worse, a handpicked captain, one of his best, had chosen this moment to defect with his boat and crew. Now the entire entourage was enroute to Florida, including the despised journalist.

Castro took a deep breath and tried to calm himself. He would eventually find the books, if not all of them, at least most of them. Those copies found would be destroyed publicly and he would prosecute all who had tried to distribute them. A few copies might remain, but fear was a potent weapon, one that he knew well how to wield. There would be examples made in order for all to understand the consequences of such conduct.

The defection of an elite patrol boat captain with his crew along with the escape of these criminals, however; these were components of a more immediate and troublesome problem. Although he had ordered more Cuban patrol boats to the scene, he knew that by the time they arrived there would be little more to do than escort the damaged craft back to port.

Now in international waters, every second brought the defectors and the cursed journalist closer to U.S. waters and the coast of Florida. They no doubt thought they were already safe in the womb of America and far from his grasp.

True, no boat could catch them, but a single MiG-23 would have no such problem. He picked up the phone and pressed the auto-dial button that would put him in direct contact with the air base commander.

# Chapter
# Thirteen

Two weeks into his assignment, Seaman Apprentice Robert Patterson was enjoying his second cup of coffee on a Monday morning in the control room of the U.S. Coast Guard's Key West operations office. His primary responsibility, one he took very seriously, consisted of monitoring marine band transmissions on a designated frequency. The fairly mundane activity was inevitably assigned to the lowest ranking person on duty. This morning, however, would prove to be anything but normal or routine.

Seaman Patterson had just raised the cup of steaming coffee to his lips when the mayday call came in. He let out a yelp when a good portion of the contents of his cup spilled down the front of his shirt. Trying to compose himself, he verified the information, then beat a path to his supervisor's office.

"Sir, we've just received a mayday transmission from an American vessel," he said, still wiping the coffee splash off the front of his uniform.

William "Big Bill" Benjamin looked up from his paper-strewn desk, his eyebrows arching over his reading glasses. He was a large man who moved slowly, but his lack of physical agility belied a sharp and quick-thinking mind. Over the course of nearly 30 years in the ranks of the U.S. Coast Guard, he figured he'd seen just about everything at least once. And a mayday transmission, while important, was nothing to spill one's coffee over.

"So?" he asked, appraising the young seaman's coffee-stained shirt.

"Sir," Patterson went on, "an American vessel identified as the *Miguel*, has three American citizens and two Cuban nationals on board. They're coming from Cuba running with one engine down. The Cuban nationals on board are asking for asylum in the United States.

"And sir, they suspect there may well be Cuban naval vessels in pursuit of them. The captain," he looked down at his notes, "one Alberto Pascual, has requested Coast Guard assistance to ensure their safe entry into U.S. waters."

"What's their current location?" asked Big Bill, adjusting his glasses.

"They're about 30 miles out, sir," Patterson said handing him the slip of paper with the specific coordinates scribbled on it.

Big Bill Benjamin sighed and cradled the phone to his ear when the young seaman blurted out, "That's not quite all, sir."

Calmly, he put the phone down and said, "Okay, let's hear it."

"Well sir, it seems that the American boat is being escorted by a Cuban Border Patrol vessel. One of the new ones, sir. According to Captain Pascual, the Cuban Border Patrol captain and his crew of eleven also wish to defect to the United States. He said something about a gun battle between the defecting patrol boat and another patrol boat out in the Straits."

"Anything else?" asked Big Bill Benjamin.

"No sir," said the seaman.

"Okay. You better sit down son, and no more coffee. Looks like we're going to have ourselves a busy little morning."

One of Big Bill's oversize fingers punched the auto-dial button on his phone console. Within two minutes after he hung up the phone, a U.S. Coast Guard surveillance aircraft that had been flying over Key Largo was diverted to new coordinates.

Fifteen minutes later, the pilot radioed that he had a visual sighting of both vessels and reported their exact coordinates. The pilot then made a low sweeping circle over *Miguel* and the Cuban patrol boat. He dialed his radio to the standard Coast Guard marine frequency and hailed the boat named *Miguel*.

"Captain," he said, "I'm confirming that you have two Cuban nationals on board and their wish is to seek asylum in the United States."

"Affirmative," answered Alberto. "The Cuban nationals are my wife and adopted child. We also have two other U.S. citizens on board and we are all looking forward to getting to Florida as soon as possible. I believe we may have some Cuban military enroute who are interested in us not reaching the U.S. mainland. I am requesting Coast Guard escort for ourselves and the Cuban patrol boat accompanying us. They've already saved us once this morning."

"Roger on that request," said the pilot. "Is the captain of the Cuban patrol boat monitoring this frequency?"

"Yes," said Carlos into his microphone, trying to remember his best English. "This is Captain Remis of the Cuban Border Guard. I wish to formally convey my intention, and that of my crew, to defect to the United States."

"I copy that," said the pilot. "To confirm your intentions, Captain, I request that you lower your guns and point them down off your port side."

The pilot watched as his request was quickly adhered to. He then gave both captains the specific course coordinates for their approach to Key West.

"A Coast Guard escort will be under way shortly," said the pilot. "They should be here within a half hour. Stay on your current course and you'll be fine."

Just then his navigator leaned forward and interrupted the pilot. "Sir," he said, not taking his eyes away from his radar screen, "we have a new situation developing. I just picked up a bogie that took off from the Cuban air base south of Havana. It's still in Cuban airspace, but it's fast and coming directly this way."

"What the hell is it?" asked the pilot suddenly becoming very serious.

"It's definitely military in nature," said the navigator. "At the speed it's moving, I'd say it's a MiG."

The navigator's words had been picked up by the pilot's headset microphone and were clearly transmitted to the radios on both the Cuban patrol boat and *Miguel*.

Alberto turned and looked at Dan with a worried expression. "We're going to need some help, amigo," he said, "and a half an hour is going to be too late."

The young MiG-23 pilot had taken off from the Cuban air base at San Antonio de los Banos, roughly 20 miles southwest of Havana, only minutes before. Thrust backwards into his seat by the force of his acceleration, he checked his instruments and struck out on a northeasterly course at full speed. The missile stores indicator in the cockpit dash confirmed that the two air-to-surface missiles beneath his wings were fully armed.

His orders could not have been more clear, nor could have they come from anyone higher in the command structure. There was no mistake about it. He was to take out both the patrol boat and the American craft, if at all possible, while they were still in international waters.

Lucky, he thought, that his aircraft had already been fitted with the air-to-surface missiles, as the usual combat stores were air-to-air missiles. MiGs were normally meant to engage other jets, not boats, but today would be an exception.

Glancing at one of the MiG's navigation screens in front of him, he adjusted his course based on the transponder coordinates beamed up to him from the Cuban patrol boat.

Defecting or not, all Cuban patrol boats were equipped with transponders that emitted a beacon on a specific identifying frequency. With the transponder guiding his course, he estimated that he would reach his target within minutes.

A phone rang at an air base in South Florida. It was answered on the first ring, since this line was designated for situations that demanded immediate responses.

The commander of the U.S. Southeast Air Defense Sector at Homestead Air Reserve Base was advised of a fast-developing situation in the Florida Straits by his old friend "Big Bill" Benjamin. There was no time for small talk between them. In less than 30 seconds they had both hung up and things began happening.

The pilots of two Florida Air National Guard F-15C fighters sprinted across the tarmac at the Homestead Air Reserve Base, their support crews scrambling. Within seconds, their engines came to life and both jets taxied to the end of the runway. They took off, afterburners blazing even in the bright morning sunlight. The jets arched over the Florida mainland, heading due southeast to the Florida Straits, toward Cuba.

On the Cuban patrol boat, Captain Carlos Rimus looked at the radar screen, as did Dan below deck on *Miguel*. They both knew that in a matter of moments a drama would play out that would determine all of their fates.

Dan wiped his brow as he intently watched a group of blips on a green circular screen: one blip came from Cuba, two blips came from the U.S. mainland; all were in a race to the center of the circular screen that indicated the position of two vessels in the Florida Straits. It looked like a dead heat to him.

Fearing the worst, Captain Rimus ordered his gunner to action, although he knew it was all but useless. The air-to-surface missiles carried on a MiG-23 far outclassed any response his twin guns could offer. But if his crew could sight the pilot before he released his lethal hardware, he would fire at the MiG. The young captain had no doubt in his mind that the pilot's orders were to sink both vessels.

Standing on the deck of *Miguel*, Alberto, Maria, Elsita and Julita heard a rumble in the distance. They waited and wondered if they would be alive to see the outcome of an episode that could be over as quickly as it began.

The MiG pilot saw the two approaching blips on his screen at the same moment that he locked onto the deserting patrol boat. An instant later, his alarm system went off indicating that the missile systems of both approaching U.S. fighters had locked on to his aircraft. He quickly computed the odds. He could perhaps fire one of his missiles, but he would not survive long enough to see it hit its target.

He made his decision in the click of a second hand. He abruptly arched away from the oncoming F-15s and the two boats that had been his targets. Only after turning away and putting several hundred yards between him and the vessels, did he release both his missiles. They splashed down into the water harmlessly.

The young pilot had decided that this mission was not worth his death on top of the deaths of those on the two vessels. There was no win possible in this situation. He would report being engaged by two U.S. fighters and, although releasing his missiles at the targets, he had missed both. He would indicate that, outnumbered two to one, he had barely been able to make it back to the base with his aircraft intact. It was a lie, but an acceptable one. And he would live to fly again.

Watching the young Cuban pilot's actions, both U.S. pilots toggled off their missiles, but stayed with him until it was clear he was returning to Cuban air space. Then they turned back and made a low pass over *Miguel* and the Cuban patrol boat.

"The bogie has gone bye-bye," the lead pilot reported over the radio to cheers in both the Southeast Air Defense Sector headquarters and the Key West Coast Guard control room. He switched his frequency to the maritime band and added for the benefit of the boats below, "Welcome to America, folks. You should be safe from here on in. Looks like you've got yourself a first-class escort en route."

They stood on the deck of *Miguel* and cheered wildly, as did the crew of the Cuban Patrol boat, when the two U.S. jets made a low pass over them. Maria hugged Dan, and then they turned and looked toward the horizon where the jets had headed. In the distance, they could see three U.S. Coast Guard ships coming toward them from the U.S. mainland.

A small group, including Maria and her boss Max Silva, had gathered around one of the television monitors in the editorial department of the *Herald* that was tuned to the Fox Network News.

"We have a breaking news story from Havana this morning and, in fact, from several cities across Cuba. It's been three weeks since celebrated journalist and author Maria Montoro made news by personally managing to deliver a few thousand copies of her book, *A Simple Tale of Truth,* to Cuba. It describes a mythical island country in which the people finally demand freedom from an oppressive king. Despite the fact that the book has been officially banned by the Castro regime and orders have been issued to burn any copies found in Cuba, the book seems to have taken on a life of its own.

"We're going live now to our Latin America correspondent, Gina Alexis, in Havana. Gina, are you there?"

"Thanks, Chris. Across this country today there have been reported work stoppages and a mounting number of peaceful protests demanding that a true democracy be instituted in Cuba. Literally thousands of citizens have taken to the streets to protest the totalitarian rule that has dominated this nation for the past 40-some years."

"Gina, you have been present at a number of historical occasions including the downfall of the Soviet Union and the collapse of the former Iron Curtain countries. How does this compare with those events?"

"I've never seen anything quite like this, Chris. I suppose one could liken it to 1989 when the Berlin Wall finally came down. It was one of those historic occasions when everything seemed to change overnight. One day it was a city divided, and the next it was a city united. And no one anticipated that it would happen peacefully.

"Something is going on here that is unprecedented. Never before have I seen so many people from all walks of life—

including shopkeepers, factory workers, and farmers—all coming together and demanding a true democracy. It's really quite remarkable. There is a sense of wonder about it all."

"What are the reactions of the police and the military?"

"That's perhaps the most amazing part. So far the police and the military have done nothing. They are just letting it happen. No one has taken up arms. It's all been completely peaceful. In fact, we have been getting reports that in some cases, the police and military personnel are actually joining the protest. Let me emphasize that this entire spontaneous event is only hours old. It is truly unfolding as we speak. I don't think any of us know exactly where it's going."

"Has there been any official response from Fidel Castro?"

"Not yet, Chris. But as you can see behind me, the crowd started gathering at dawn today at the plaza here outside the Presidential Palace, and it continues to grow. I understand there are similar gatherings in towns and cities across this country. Some sort of official reaction will be needed very soon."

They continued to gather throughout the day. By early evening, the plaza outside the Presidential Palace in Havana was overflowing. They stood and they waited. Despite the size of the crowd, the plaza remained eerily silent. It was a silence of defiance unknown in Cuba since Castro's takeover.

In the ornate office with the balcony that looked out over the plaza, the last rays of sunshine came in through the glass panels of the closed doors and spilled long slants of light across his desk. In the center of his desk lay a copy of a children's book.

Castro stood in the shadows. He did not move toward the balcony, but gazed out the window in silence. Dreading the moment, he waited to hear the music.

One morning the people of the little island gathered together, first one, then two, then a hundred, then more... until all the people of the little island stood as one. Together, they stood outside the palace in silence and waited.

The aging king, who had ruled so long with an iron fist, shouted down at them from the balcony, "Why do you not go back to work? I order you to disperse!"

But the people merely stood and waited. They waited through the day until the shadows became long and dusk approached.

"How dare you not heed my orders?" he shouted down to them, but there was only silence in return.

Angered, the king finally ordered his knights to disperse them, but the knights would not harm the people. To his horror, he watched as one by one, the knights left the palace to join the people and waited with them.

As the sun began to set, the aging king stood on the balcony of the palace and looked out. As far as he could see were people, all standing and waiting.

And then a strange thing happened. A young girl started to play a flute and the people found it beautiful, and it was as if they heard music for the first time.

As they listened, they remembered all they had lost and they knew their wait was over, that the island would be theirs again, as it had always been theirs to give or take away.

The king, discovering that he no longer had any power over them, fled from the palace and the island that was never really his, but was something given to him by the people, like a gift, like love. And now they had taken it back, the gift tarnished, the love soured.

Once again there was a magical island surrounded by clear blue waters, where tall palm trees grew and beautiful music could be heard during the day and night.

# Epilogue

Maria crested the hill outside of Victoria de las Tunas on horseback. The sun was high in the Cuban sky. She had been riding fast, but now she slowed as she made her way through the lush green pasture toward a stately plantation home. Not far behind her, Dan came over the hill, also on horseback. He shared his saddle with young Julita, who was obviously enjoying the ride immensely.

"So, this is where you were born?" asked Dan as he caught up with her. "It's a beautiful country, a beautiful home."

"The house has been in the family since the 1800s. My great great grandparents lived here. And it's the house where my parents were married," Maria said.

Dan looked at it appreciatively, admiring the proud old plantation home that was framed by a white fence. Finally, he glanced at his watch and said, "We'd better get a move on or we'll be late."

By the time Dan and Maria reached the city, crowds had already gathered in and around the town square and the central park where the old statue of Maria's great great great grandfather stood, Vicente García, known as *El Leon De Santa Rita*, "The Lion of St. Rita. His victory over the Spaniards in the Ten Year War that began in 1868 had given Victoria de las Tunas its name and its initial independence.

A band was playing a Latin melody and a festive energy permeated the summer air. Many people had already filled the rows of chairs that had been arranged in the square, while others stood on the sidewalks and grass. On a podium erected in the center of the square were several more rows of chairs, some reserved for local officials, and others for Maria's family and friends.

As she and Dan approached the crowded square, people started applauding and waving, and the band broke into a new song. The bandleader quickly took the microphone saying, "In honor of this wonderful occasion, we will play for the first time a new original piece that we have composed, "Viva Maria!" The announcement was greeted with huge applause.

Working their way through the crowd, Maria recognized many familiar faces of friends and family. Her nieces and nephews— Lynn, Justin, Michael, Kameron, Alec and Erin— the children of her brothers who had fled with her so many years before to the safety of America, sat fidgeting nearby. Her Godparents, Maria Antonia and Edgardo, who had traveled all the way from Havana, sat in the second row of chairs.

The sun was bright and Maria put her hand over her eyebrows to see the crowd better. Then she stopped abruptly and clutched Dan's arm.

"What's wrong?" asked Dan concerned.

Out of the corner of her eye, Maria thought she saw the figure of Fernando García near the back of the crowd. But that would be impossible for he had died so long ago. She peered intently, but he had disappeared. How strange, she thought. It had seemed so real for that instant, as if he were standing there alive and well and smiling once again. And she reminded herself again that Victoria de las Tunas was an old city, perhaps visited sometimes by old souls.

As she reached the podium, her cousin Sandra, who had remained in Las Tunas all these years, kissed and hugged her so hard she almost lost her balance as she and Dan stepped onto the stage. Julita let go of Maria's hand and ran to Alberto and Elsita, who were already seated next to Maria's and Dan's parents. Maria's father Miguel waved to her and blew her a kiss. Elena, finally putting away her cell phone, motioned her and Dan toward the last empty seats in the center of the front row.

The mayor, a rotund man of medium height with a balding head and a beard, straightened his white suit as he stepped to the microphone. He surveyed the crowd for a moment, waiting for the cheers to subside, before clearing his throat and beginning his address.

"We have gathered today in celebration of a true hero," he said to a new chorus of cheers and enthusiastic applause. "For all you have done," the mayor continued, "and for what you have encouraged us to do, we honor you today, Maria Montoro.

"Who is to say that sometimes a fairy tale can't come true? Who is to say that the truth found in a child's heart and a child's eyes cannot be captured in the minds and actions of adults? Who is to say that by believing in something we cannot make it so?"

The crowd applauded again and Maria smiled and blushed. A gentle wind blew through her hair and rustled the skirts of the women sitting on the podium.

"It is my honor," the mayor continued, "to dedicate a lasting tribute today to our Maria, who dared to speak the truth and made us believe it could be so."

With that he pulled back a shroud revealing a bronze statue of a beautiful young girl standing at water's edge, her arms raised. The crowd stood and applauded and the band played again.

Some thought the statue was meant to portray the young girl who played music in Maria's book. Others said it bore a unique likeness to Maria herself at that age. The sculptor, a local artist of national reputation, would never say. In the end, perhaps it did not matter, for whatever one might see in the statue, the words etched into its pedestal left no doubt. In simple block letter it read: "In honor of Maria Montoro, who showed us the truth, so we could find freedom and liberty."

The ceremony ended, but many in the crowd still lingered in the square, wishing Maria well as she stood next to Dan holding his hand. The gathering could have been mistaken for a family reunion or a wedding reception. In fact, one could not help but notice the wedding ring she now wore, and several people commented that they had never seen her look more happy or beautiful.

When it came time to go, Elsita looked for Julita, calling her name. She finally found her sitting in front of the statue. Julita pointed up at it and said, "I know who the statue looks like, Mami. It's an angel."

Elsita smiled and took her hand. "Really? Tell me why you think so." she said.

"Because the nice old man told me," said Julita. "The one dressed all in white. And he gave me his hankie, see?"

Elsita looked down at the white cotton handkerchief grasped firmly in her child's hand.

"He said it was a present and that I could keep it. Can I show Aunt Maria?"

Elsita nodded and watched as Julita ran across the green grass to show Maria her precious treasure.